June 28, 2012

Doris,
   I hope you enjoy your stay 'at "The Beach". Take care.
        Holly B.

Additional copies are available at Amazon.com keywords: "The River Beach"

# The River Beach

Holly Bittle

For Bob,
(whom is both Jacob and Bobby)
His painful and constant hard work
allowed me precious time with our children,
and time to write.

## Chapter One

The River sometimes brought 40 thousand people per day. Mostly they came from Philadelphia, traveling 34 miles South East aboard a magnificent fleet of ferry ships. They came to enjoy a day away from the city in rural Salem County, New Jersey. The attraction was not a day in the country. It was the world class amusements at the Riverview Beach Park. The thirty acre park was filled with every type of whirring ride mankind had yet built. There were roller coasters both large and small. There were rides that could swing you up, spin you, drop you or make you fly. Visitors enjoyed a fun house, a glass house, colossal slides both wet and dry, games of skill and chance, a man made lake with paddle boats, an olympic-sized pool and the sandy river beach for bathing, a skating rink and dance hall, a large elegant restaurant, and of course the food vendors. The sandwiches were said to be world class. The smell of the food alone was worth the trip. The hot river breeze air was full with music. The park was an enchanting wonderland of physical indulgence.

The year was 1951, the Second World War had been over for six years, the first of the baby boom generation were just beginning their school years. It was the year that the first sports games would be televised in color. The first long distance phone call would be made from New Jersey to California without the aide of an operator. The sultry voices of Rosemary Clooney and Nat King Cole were the sounds of the day. Girls had their hair shorter and styled, they wore full skirts that came down past the knee. Men took off their hats indoors and were polite around ladies. The art of conversation was still alive and well.

At Riverview Beach Park, the time of the ferries was coming to an end. A massive construction project was underway within site of the park. It was a mile long structure that we now know as the Delaware Memorial Bridge. By the end of August the bridge would connect car traffic from New Jersey to Delaware.

It was a summer day, the first of July. Georgia Sparks stood inside a booth which existed almost in the smack dab center of that magical park. She worked in one of the little sandwich huts. She acted as both a waitress and a short order cook. There were four stools lining the front of the booth where customers could sit at the counter. Fragrances from her grill joined others to produce the world class aromas that visitors were raving about. Even Georgia herself was something to see. She was definitely one of the prettiest girls who resided in Lower Penns

Neck. She barely wore any makeup and only fooled with her hair on occasion. She was one of those natural beauties. She stood 5'4", with thick medium brown hair that she kept longer than most girls. Her hair naturally curled just on the ends. Georgia had an angular athletic body, and beautifully sculptured nose and jaw. Being a target of envy, Georgia only had a handful of close friends. Her temperament was sweet and steady. She was wise far beyond her 19 years.

Working in the park as a teenager had been a right of passage in Lower Penns Neck for over twenty years. Georgia had expected to find herself here her entire childhood.

It was a mild day for July, but sunny. Georgia kept looking at her hands. She had on nail polish for the first time. It was red. Her younger sister and two of their friends had decided to try it. It looked so strange and exotic. She couldn't say whether or not she liked it.

Georgia raised a polished hand to her forehead and squinted to see out into the park. Paddle boats drifted gently on the lake amid the rocking and swinging amusements. Joyful music ebbed and flowed. Her older sister, Doris, was approaching with her exuberant pair of children in tow. A smile revealed Georgia's perfect teeth.

Doris's wedding, the birth of her babies, and the pomp surrounding each, had been the most exciting points of Georgia's school years. She had been Doris's bridesmaid at only thirteen. There were many times during her teen years that Georgia admired her big sister so much that she couldn't tear her eyes off of her. Georgia still felt that way sometimes. Now those feelings centered mostly on the perfect little brother and sister pair.

"Hey lady, we'll have two grilled ham and swiss," Doris smiled from under a wide brimmed hat. She had darker shorter brunette hair. Doris had the same handsome nose and jaw.

"Sure thing lady," Georgia answered, then bent to get some meat and cheese from a cooler. Doris sat in one of the center stools, the children climbed up on either side. They were both blonde with painfully cute faces that you just wanted to pinch. Doris was a proud woman and she barely let those two out of the house unless they were perfectly groomed and strait.

"Did you know that we're coming for dinner tonight? Daddy's got some big news he wants to share with the whole family."

"Oh, no, they didn't mention it at breakfast this morning," Georgia replied, "I wonder what the news could be?"

Doris' daughter spoke up, "brother's got a loose tooff." Their names were Thomas and Jessie, but they called each other 'brother' and 'sister'. It only made them more adorable.

"He does, well let me see," Georgia cooed. She loved being their Aunt; it made her feel so grown up.

After a typical work day, Georgia waited for her younger sister in their usual spot. It was the river side of the Tilt-a-whirl, on the North West corner of the park. When they worked similar shifts, the two always walked home together.

There was a continuous happy noise to the park. It was the music, the chatter and howls of the visitors, and rhythmic groans of machinery; the noise had been particularly draining that day. Georgia couldn't wait to get home. She saw Olive approaching. Georgia could see that Olive was upset from fifteen feet away. Her lips were pressed together and she was clenching her jaw. She walked with purpose. Olive was petite and cute, with medium brown hair and freckles. She was better at fixing her hair than Georgia was, but by this hour her hair was straggly.

The girls liked to walk along the River, although it would have been a shorter walk to take Broadway home. Georgia and Olive, although almost two years apart in age, were each other's closest friend and confidant. Olive didn't embarrass herself by popping off in public. She waited until they were on North River Drive to tell Georgia what the problem was. They were a block away from the park before the constant 'crowd noise' began to relent. Olive took a deep breath.

"I cannot, *cannot*, be cousins with that low life Martha anymore!," she finally declared. Georgia hated to see her sister upset. She was obviously very hurt. Olive would not say something like that without a valid reason.

Martha was a loud mouth, and not very lady like. Although she was very sensitive and cared a lot about what others thought, she thought nothing of talking bad about others publicly. She was always giving long explanations for her actions as if she was actually convincing people to see things her way. She had not figured out that people just didn't care enough about what she is saying to argue with her. It was as if she couldn't handle people having their own opinions. Quite pathetic.

"Ug! Georgia how can we possibly be related to that ridiculous mess!?"

"Maybe Uncle Walter is not her real Daddy," Georgia giggled trying to lighten the mood, then added "what now, Honey?"

They walked slowly with the River on their left. The bridge was in view, but the girls did not look at it as they walked this time.

"I was having lunch with Agnes, Margaret, Shirley and *her*, and she embarrassed me so badly with her.. her.. *rudeness*! She loudly admitted to wishing that Cathy and Barnie would split up! Georgia, her actual words were, - and -I -quote, 'Barnie and Cathy are so happy about her pregnancy it is ridiculous! When he leaves her for somebody prettier I am going to *LAUGH*!' Have you ever heard anything so crass in your life!? *She* didn't even *know* why we were looking at her with our mouths hanging open!"

"Well, that's Martha for ya. The woman has something wrong with her brain," Georgia responded coolly. "That is exactly why she hasn't got a husband, she's certainly pretty enough."

The girls stopped now and Georgia put her arms around her sister. As they hugged Olive spouted into her sister's hair, "What did Barnie and Cathy do to her anyway?"

"She is probably just mad because they are happy, some folks actually don't like for others to be happy. Don't try to figure her out, Honey, you are a good person and therefore Martha doesn't think like you," Georgia offered. They started walking again holding hands.

"But doesn't she make you furious; she is family to us, talking like that!" Olive said a little shaky. Georgia responded quickly,

"No, I feel sorry for her."

"Sorry for her!," Olive shot back more loudly than she meant to. Georgia only squeezed her sister's hand.

"Yeah, on account of she is miserable. Happy people don't attack others like that, miserable people do." Because Olive was so shaken and hurt, Georgia felt a strong urge to defend her.

"Don't you worry about her anymore my Sweetheart, I'll take care of her for you –at the forth of July picnic."

"You promise?," Olive almost broke down.

"Promise," Georgia said, she immediately started searching for the right thing to do or say.

## Chapter Two

The Sparks family lived in a large brick cape on Cherry Street in the Central Park neighborhood. The rooms were spacious as was the yard. It was three blocks North of the park, and about a quarter mile off the River. John Sparks had been working at the Deepwater I.E. Dupont plant for going on thirty years now. He provided a comfortable living for his family. Jean Sparks was a cheerful and loving wife and mother. She didn't overly concern herself with fashion or vanity, but Jean had once been a beauty who could knock the breath out of a man from a full twenty feet away. Many men had envied John, a seemingly average man, for the striking beauty of his wife. These days Jean was fully content concerning herself with the affairs of her household.

Georgia and Olive entered the side door. The house was cleaner then usual and filled with the wonderful smell of chili and corn bread. Jean was putting a leaf in the dinning room table. She was wearing a white apron and her dark blonde hair looked a little more special today. Georgia remembered the special dinner, and Daddy's surprise. Olive's drama had caused Georgia to forget.

"Mother, dinner smells great." Olive chimed, obviously feeling better.

"Why don't you girls get cleaned up right away, and then help me with dinner. Doris and Gabe are going to be here around four." Their Mother had skipped her usual, 'how was your day'. All three of the Sparks girls had adopted their Mother's grace. She had only a handful of times spoken ill of anyone, and only got upset at very dire situations. Although her mood was always light, Jean had earned the respect of family and friends.

The two girls went upstairs to the one large bedroom they shared. It was, in fact, the entire upstairs of the cape house. They returned in fresh clothes.

Gabor, Doris and their kids arrived at four. Doris was wearing lipstick and a broad smile. She brought dessert, strawberry shortcake. The kids were in fresh clothes. Jessie's hair was braided. Gabor, a quiet man, spoke first, "Jean, Dinner smells wonderful."

* * *   * * *

Gabor was the youngest son of Hungarian immigrants. He had spent four years in Europe during the war, which was undoubtedly the reason for his occasional periods of withdrawal. They say that what doesn't kill you only makes you stronger. In the case of Gabor and many others like him, that old saying just isn't so. Just as often, what doesn't kill you leaves you wrecked. He never spoke about the war, not even to Doris.

He had gotten through that miserable period by living in a fantasy state. Whenever it was possible for his mind to drift away from his circumstances he visualized the family he wanted to have when he returned home. He visualized the children in detail. Gabor had a pleasant childhood and adored his own father. More than anything he wanted to be a father himself. And so Thomas and Jessie didn't come about in the usual biological way. Her pregnancies and deliveries were typical, so of course nobody knew the difference. People very seldom do. This is not common knowledge but sometimes children are actually willed into existence. Because Gabor had focused so much on the children he wanted to have, pictured them in such detail and with such emotion, he had actually manifested them. He pictured a blonde boy with blue eyes like his own. He imagined how strong the little tike would be and the games they would play together. As father and son. He even knew how his little face would wrinkle up when he smiled. And how his laugh sounded. He pictured a little girl with large brown doe eyes. Eyes that could project love right into you. He knew how her little walk would go. And how she would sometimes hold out her hand, fingers tight together, when she spoke. He had created all the details of these children, and he knew them well. These images gave him the strength to want to live his life while seeing and experiencing horrific things. Because he focused so much thought on these children he actually, through Doris, brought them to life.

    Doris had met Gabor, about a week after he returned home from overseas. He was falling out of a bus, drunk as a skunk. Doris took him home where Jean helped her take care of him. They love to tell this story. The two women took care of him for a day and a half before they even knew his name. Doris and Gabor were married within three months.

* * *  * * *

The four women helped get dinner on the table. Everyone chatted pleasantly and ate while waiting for John's announcement. Georgia was now in a blissful mood. The chili and corn bread was heaven after her day of work, and this dinner had the special feel of a holiday. It was like a holiday that had snuck up on her by surprise. She enjoyed the warmth of having the whole family around her.

Finally he began, "Jacob came to see me on Saturday." Georgia raised her beautiful brows. Her boyfriend, Jacob who lived in Woodstown, shared a work truck with his father. He only came to Lower Penns Neck two or three times a week. Georgia was surprised that he had come to town without her knowing.

"He described to me how much he cared for Georgia and I guess it's no surprise that he asked my permission for her hand in marriage." Olive squealed, Georgia just smiled her eyes darted from her Daddy to Olive. She didn't know what to say or feel.

John went on, "Of course I said yes you know how I feel about Jacob. He did have another surprise for Georgia and I'm not keeping it." He turned to Georgia, "As far I'm concerned you are still my girl, for the moment anyway, and *I'm* going to be the one to tell you this news." John had practiced this announcement; he turned to Georgia and took her hand. "Do you remember that large house on the corner of North Main Street and Elm, the one Jacob's family has been working on? He took you to see it once didn't he?"

"Yes", Georgia squeaked. He took her to see his 'work site' on what was probably the second of her five trips to Woodstown.

"Well, it belongs to the Layton's now. The family they were building it for had to move out West abruptly. Suddenly Georgia sucked in a breath; she knew where he might be going with this. "It's yours, Honey, he's going to surprise you with it as an engagement gift."

"Oh, Daddy, Daddy, are you sure?! I mean, are they sure?!", Georgia stammered.

"He was sure when he told me. After I spoke to old Brucie Layton I decided I was going to be the one to surprise my girl."

By now Jean, Olive, and Doris were on their feet and moving toward Georgia. Olive embraced her first, then her mother, then Doris. Georgia was recalling everything she could remember about the large house. It seemed to her like it was a mansion. She called it a mansion before she had the wherewithal to be humble. So from that moment on the Sparks women began referring to it as 'the mansion'. They chattered ceaselessly, it was one of the most exciting times the four of them could remember. John was glad that he had decided to tell Jacob's secret, he loved seeing his girls happy. He told them that one day, years in the future, they will tell Jacob that his surprise had been let out of the bag early.

Jacob was a hard working and admirable man. He had been sawing, hammering, and creating with an almost inhuman energy since his early teens. His physical capacity for work was truly amazing. At only 28 he may have actually deserved that mansion. He undoubtedly built most of it. His coworkers couldn't begin to keep up with him. Jacob was not strikingly handsome, but a good looking strong young man, and as even tempered as they get. He would take good care of his wife. Jacob was also itching to become a father. Georgia had met him during the previous summer. John had hired Layton Construction Company to build his garage. Jacob came, he was the foreman. There were three others with him.

Once they got to know each other a little bit, Jacob recognized Georgia as the precious treasure she was. The boys she had grown up with in town hadn't paid her much extra attention. Maybe that was because they were used to her. Maybe it was because they found her to be too prude. Georgia was flattered by the way she struck Jacob when they met, and how he couldn't wait to show his father how pretty she was. His father agreed. She grew to love him. He was respectful to her and wanted to take care of her. What more could she want?

* * *   * * *

Upon hearing about the 'mansion' Doris had been quieter than the other two women. It wasn't because she didn't like the idea of her younger sister moving 10 miles away. This was one of those times when it was just hard to be happy for Georgia. Their mother's mother, MeeMom, had once said that the biggest problem Georgia would have with others was jealousy. She was only 15 at that time but her gentle, infallibly optimistic nature was apparent. MeeMom's prediction was right. Georgia never would realize that her sister Doris was jealous at all. Not only did Georgia think too highly of her older sister to believe that she would have those feelings, but Georgia always felt that Doris had quite a bit to be thankful for herself. Even at that time, Georgia would have rightly traded that mansion for two perfect children such as Doris's.

Doris and Gabor stayed until close to their children's bedtime. Everyone enjoyed the mood of the dinner party. After everything had been cleaned up, Georgia and Olive went up to their room. They always went to bed early. That night the girls had much to talk about. Olive was genuinely happy for her big sister. In their upstairs bedroom rain beat loudly on their ceiling. There was no attic above them, and so rain was always loud up there. It was super cozy. The storm clouds that were still accumulating were a sharp contrast to the cheerful chatter below. The small lamp on the table between their beds cast a warm glow. Georgia had just realized that she would miss sharing this room with Olive. Saying so made Olive realize she would miss her sister being there.

"You won't even be in Lower Penn's anymore." Olive spoke slowly, suddenly not cheerful. "I'll be up here all alone at night. You won't be here at dinner –or to walk home with me after work." Georgia brought her pillow over to Olive's bed and lay down next to her sister. Olive didn't want to say anymore. As lonely as her thoughts were she didn't want to spoil things. Georgia could somehow feel her sister's hurt. It was a pain near her stomach. She thought for a long time under those tapping rain drops before she spoke.

"Olive do you remember what we learned about the Jewish people who had been taken to the concentration camps?"

"Yes," she remembered but it was something she did not want to hear or know about.

"All those horrible things really really happened to a lot of people." Georgia was making her sister think about it. "Children where taken away from their families people lived in horrendous suffering only to die awful deaths. They had feelings just the same as ours and they where ripped from their families and their lives, and endured gruesome torment. Those things really happened to real folks like us, -like Mother and Daddy."

"Ug, why are we talking about this!?," Olive moaned.

"I know it is going to be really hard for you to let me go but just remember the Jews in those camps. If you think about them you'll know that nothing bad has ever happened in your life." Georgia felt a little ridiculous after she said that, she didn't mean to be so dramatic. Georgia would soon forget that she ever said that. Olive, however, would hang onto that little nugget for life.

## Chapter Three

The next day Georgia was starry eyed in her sandwich booth. She wondered how Jacob would ask her. He probably wouldn't think of any spectacular way of giving her the ring. That just wouldn't be like Jacob. Georgia concluded that he would probably say something simple and romantic while down on one knee.

It was a pretty day. It would seem like all was fine and good. Georgia, a deserving young woman would be married to a deserving young man. So all was fine and good except that today was Tuesday. *He* had been showing up for a sandwich regularly on every Tuesday and Saturday for over two months. This thorn in Georgia's perfect side was a mysterious Italian from Philadelphia. The mere sight of this man gripped Georgia by her studious diligent little soul. She supposed that he had some feelings about her too. There were a dozen sandwich shacks almost identical to this one dotting the park, yet he kept showing up at hers.

They only spoke casually and really only when he spoke first. Georgia did not have much experience in these matters; she didn't know what was appropriate. She did not know how to proceed in this little game or whatever it was so she resigned to aloofness.

The gun she saw in his waistband one afternoon coupled with his large billfold lead her to believe that his business in the park was criminal. Bobby, if that really was his name, seemed to be more serious than the general mood of the crowd. He was dressed nicer too. He had dark skin, and thick dark hair that he kept combed back, it cured slightly into finger waves. He had small gorgeous brown eyes, and a handsome jaw. His mouth was incredible. Once Georgia had been staring at his mouth wondering what it would be like to kiss him. That was right before he winked at her and that wink was an instant strike to her chest. The man could cause her chest pain with a wink. She couldn't imagine what it would be like if he touched her.

Georgia had her eye out that day, expecting Bobby. She fried chopped steaks and put together an occasional grilled ham and cheese. She didn't have many customers that day maybe it was getting too hot out for people to feel like eating.

Georgia's mind drifted and she didn't stop herself from thinking over all the 'lunches' that her and Bobby had spent together. When she first saw him she was immediately struck by his eyes when he looked at her. She couldn't figure out why. He was extraordinarily attractive in his expensive looking suit, but it wasn't like she had never seen a good looking man before. During this first visit Georgia had asked Bobby where he was from and he said;

"South Philly, I come to the park regularly on business." Bobby quickly changed the subject. He seemed to be attracted to her too. She sensed that he actually cared what she thought of him. She was sorry she had left the house without her lipstick.

"This is excellent. You are a good cook. I like that in a girl." Bobby pointed at her with the sandwich as he spoke. Georgia noticed the gold chain that was partially tucked into his collar and the large ring on his right hand. She couldn't remember having seen a man wear jewelry other than a wedding band.

"Well, thank you Sir, I try my best." Georgia responded.

"Please, call me Bobby," he had an air about him. When he asked you to do something you'd tend to do it.

"Bobby," she said.

"You're a good kid." This time pointed his napkin at her, "I'll be back to see you sometime."

Bobby left her an extra five dollar bill. It doubled the tip money she had made that week.

On his third visit Bobby had asked Georgia what her name was.

"Georgia," she said,"Georgia Anne Sparks."

"Georgia, I like that. Is that a family name?" He was being as polite as he could.

"My father spent some time working in the south after he finished high school. Something in Georgia impressed him enough to name me after it."

She always meant to ask her Daddy about this again. She had asked about ten years ago and he said he would tell her someday, when she was older.

"Do you have any brothers or sisters?," Bobby asked. He was wiping his mouth with a napkin. He was a neat eater.

"I have two sisters, one older and one younger," she replied. She thought to herself, 'Wow, he is really interested in me?'

"Are your sisters both as gorgeous as you are?," Bobby asked. Then she thought, 'Oh, my goodness! What do I say?!'

"I'd like to think so," Georgia said with a beautiful smile.

Bobby laughed out loud.

"Well, your parents must be very proud!'

He had been wearing a dark blue suit that day and looked sharp as always.

When Bobby spoke to Georgia it seemed like he seemed to have some genuine interest in her beyond just a physical attraction. Bobby didn't strike her as any stranger to attractive women. This was one of the most remarkable things about him. Georgia couldn't figure out why a guy like that would care what she thought or be that interested in her.

Bobby's usual time came and went. Georgia was working the closing shift that day. She was just scolding herself for even caring whether or not he showed. After all she was practically an engaged woman. Jacob and her future in Woodstown is what she should be thinking about. She had so many appropriate reasons to be happy, the large house on Main Street to begin with. Georgia pulled her stool out from under the counter and sat inside the booth. The sky over the River was beautiful today. She wondered about beautiful skies over her wedding day, over her future house in Woodstown, over her with her own children. Warm early spring with her own children in the green back yard. Easter egg hunts and beautiful little girl dresses.

A gaggle of teenage boys passed by. Then she saw Bobby. A small shock of something shot down her body. He looked as good as ever, and he was headed quickly her way. To Georgia's surprise the breath taking Italian strode right past the counter to the side of the booth, he swung open the door, entered and crouched behind the counter!

She sucked in her breath and started with, "What on earth.." Her heart was now in her throat.

"Shhh, keep quiet." He ordered. Georgia looked around at the passersby. Nobody seemed to notice anything strange. He must have looked as if he belonged going into that door! Georgia's next thought was how glad she was that she looked extra fetching that day. Then she promptly scolded herself again.

"Did anybody see me come in?," he whispered.

"No, I don't think so," Georgia responded quietly. She knelt down, and lifted the lid of the cooler, pretending to be busy with it.

"What on earth is going on?" She was close to him and it was exciting.

"Sorry, Peaches but I am staying until dark." He was fooling with something inside his jacket pocket. She noticed what a fine jacket it was. After a pause he added, "My business here isn't exactly legal."

Just then Georgia realized there was a young couple standing at her counter. He was a tall blonde. She was pretty with dark hair and eyes. Georgia had to ask them to repeat their order, she was in such shock. They didn't mind, they were having the time of their lives. Once she had her back to them she forgot how to prepare the food; she just stood there for a moment at the grill. The couple was chatting and didn't notice how distracted she was. Surely they hadn't noticed the criminal under her counter. They each tried one of her famous grilled ham sandwiches and complemented her lavishly. Georgia managed to be polite. It took them forever to leave.

Georgia started cleaning the grill and striating up early. She needed to make extra time tonight. She wanted to be able to spend some time dealing with this man without anyone noticing her being late to get home. Finally, Georgia was fairly certain there was nobody around who might approach her booth. She knelt under the counter next to him. Bobby was cross-legged, his hat was cocked. Her eyes locked on his before she was even comfortably seated.

"How do you plan on getting out of here?," was all Georgia could think to ask. Her voice came out different than she had ever heard it.

He smiled a devastating smile, "When can you come back to see me?"

The poor girl was speechless for a good thirty seconds. She just stared at him. His face had an even greater effect up close. He didn't seem to be surprised or bothered by her lack of words. Georgia was paralyzed, while trying to figure out how being a foot away from gorgeous Bobby could feel comfortable and electrifying at the same time. Maybe not electrifying -burning.

"I can stay for a while now but I can't be seen with you." The game was over. Maybe they had both won.

"Of course not," he answered "you won't be seen with me." He could have said anything at all and still been in charge of her. It didn't even need to make sense. Georgia was at a loss. She figured that she should say something. She spoke very slowly and softly. Neither of them could tear their gaze from the other.

"I just learned that my boyfriend, Jacob Layton, is going to propose soon. We will be living in Woodstown, it's ten miles away."

"He is a smart man," came Bobby's cool reply, "you are an incredibly special girl." If she didn't stop looking at him she might have totally lost it. Finally she broke his gaze to look down at her right hand. His hand was cradling hers. She sucked in a breath and raised her hand slowly. The touch did not break. Their finger tips were now pressed together. She gently looked from his face to their hands. She had surely never felt like this before. He was intent on her. Their hands touched and embraced for a long time and that was more than enough. Just looking at each other was enough. At least five minutes passed as they sat like that. Both understood that they would be seeing each other again. The next touch was only that Georgia leaned her forehead onto his. She had gotten to the point where she had to choose between forcing herself to be comfortable or darting out of there like a rabbit. Now that the gaze had been broken she found words again.

"How will you get back to the city?"

"I won't go back until tomorrow. I'll have to spend the night on the beach."

"I'll come back," she said without thinking first, and then added quickly, "I'll bring you a picnic blanket." She fixed him a drink from a pitcher kept in the cooler. Georgia wondered if she was really serving a drink to gorgeous Bobby under the counter, was *this* really happening?

Now most people when faced with this degree of physical urgency would not dream of walking away, but Georgia's self control was quite something. She was able to keep a handle on what was important. She would not be caught with this man.

"I have to go now I'm sure my sister is waiting for me," she muttered quickly. She grabbed his arm and smiled. Whatever it was they shared was still there.

"I promise I'll come back. It might be very late, but I'll come back."

Bobby grabbed Georgia's other arm and pulled her close. His mouth was near her neck. "I'll be on the beach I'd wait forever for you," came his reply. She could hear his breath and she would never forget it.

Georgia straitened herself and left the booth. After about twenty steps she felt like throwing out her arms and doing a twirl. The sights and sounds of the park were wonderful now, exciting, like when she was small, everything was wonderful. She knew that her face did not look normal. She tried hard to change to a very casual expression as she walked toward her sister. Georgia's walk through the crowd seemed to be in slow motion. The lights and music were amazing. Finally, there was Olive near the Tilt-a-whirl. Familiar Olive, the same as ever. It didn't seem like she had been waiting long.

Through the park's speakers a recording of Hank Williams was playing. Georgia hummed along, although she secretly preferred rhythm and blues over country music.

*I went down to the river to watch the fish swim by.*
*But I got down to the river*
*so lonesome I wanted to die, Oh Lord!*
*And then I jumped in the river*
*but the doggone river was dry.*

The girls were on their own for dinner tonight. Their Mother had told them so. Jean was glad she could finally do that occasionally. The girls were practically grown and working who-knows-what shift at the park. Georgia had to force herself to stay focused and chat as they walked. Olive had to repeat herself twice. Of course Olive thought that her older sister was lost in a day dream about the mansion. She sure would be. The sisters met up with their friends, Margaret and Shirley. The four girls together shared two shakes and two large plates of cheese fries. They often shared, sitting close together on one of the parks many large picnic tables. The music was loud where they sat and Georgia was glad. It was helping her hide her new emotions. Olive had to be the one to tell Margaret and Shirley about the upcoming proposal.

Somehow for Georgia the salt and cheese tasted even better after spending that time with Bobby. Everything was amazing now. He was amazing. She had to twice stop herself from beginning to tell Olive what had happened.

Bobby had only stayed in the booth until he was sure that Georgia was out of sight. He was not a man who needed to hide from the park guards. The guards knew well who he was and steered clear of Bobby Mano. They had no intention of interfering in his business. It wasn't as if he was violent. After all if people wanted to involve themselves in gambling that was their business. That's what the guards said to each other anyway. In reality, they didn't care to open up a can of Joe Ida's Philly mafia worms.

So it was illegal "book keeping" that brought him. He had been coming to the park twice a week because one of his four high bidding clients always wanted to meet him regularly on Tuesday. The others he met on Saturday. He was planning on encouraging his Tuesday client to meet on Saturdays as well, but then he met Georgia. Suddenly making money became his secondary motivation for making the regular trips to Riverview Beach.

He had been thinking about her often. There was something about her. Something steady and pure that came naturally. Other girls seemed fake compared to her. Bobby had been with scores of attractive women, but not one of them compared to Georgia. She was real or something. He couldn't quite get his mind around it. Already he had feelings for her. He wondered about this, it was incredible to him. This thing with Georgia made him feel out of control. Bobby was very uncomfortable with that part of it. I mean he really did have things to do. He didn't need to hide under a counter for an hour, and spend the night on the beach. Luckily he had made dinner plans with a pair of old friends. They would spend hours at the Mariner eating, drinking and reliving old times. However Bobby probably would have stayed the night at the park even if he didn't have those plans. He *had* to spend time with her, and the little ploy he pulled was all he could think of to ensure some time with her. It was not his most ingenious scheme, but he only had to fool a sheltered 19-year old.

Imagine it, Bobby Mano head over heals for a South Jersey bumpkin! Was he out of his mind? 'I'll wait forever for you?!', was he having a mental crisis?! He shook his head. All he was sure of at that point was that he had to have the sweet little thing. He could already feel his fingers running over her skin. But more importantly, Bobby needed to flush this thing out. Why would he care this much for a bumpkin he barely knew? The boyfriend Georgia had mentioned was not a concern. If anything the fact that she was in a relationship supported his notion that she was sheltered and hadn't been with different men. Bobby had easily stolen women from other men before. This only added to the excitement. It gave her a sporting chance.

## Chapter Four

All evening Georgia had no doubt that she would come back. She had to. It was difficult for her to focus on anything else. She had spoken to Jacob on the phone, and it was great to hear his voice. But he was tired and she was distracted and so their conversation was short. He wished her a good night and told her he would be thinking of her. It was the same sort of thing they always said to each other. She was comforted by his words, and politely wished him a good night.

Her parents had noticed how distant Georgia was. They assumed it was because of the huge life changes she was facing. Jean and John had even discussed Georgia's behavior with Olive briefly, after Olive mentioned something about Georgia's demeanor. However nobody was more than mildly concerned.
Georgia was trying her best to behave normally, and she did well given the circumstances.

Georgia had showered, shaved, and carefully powdered herself with melon scented powder. She enjoyed being alone with her thoughts in the cozy bathroom. Georgia's plan was only to sneak out when everyone was asleep. Once upstairs in their bedroom Georgia spoke very little to Olive. She was trying to bore her to sleep and then will her to sleep. The poor girl. Georgia lay there listening to Olive breath. Her heart thumped in her chest. There was no way sneaking out to see him was a good idea. There was no way she could stop from going.

Moonlight streamed in through their café style curtains. The clock on her nightstand said 9:02. She remembered what it was like to be close to him. His eyes, his expression, the electricity in the touch. Georgia lay perfectly still while remembering her short time with Bobby and lost herself in every move. An hour must have passed. Nope, only 9:20. At least Olive was asleep.

Finally, a little after 10 pm, her parents were sound asleep too. She slipped on a white sleeveless blouse and a skirt. After she had her lipstick perfectly in place, she went silently out of the back door. The sky was clear and the air was comfortable. Her mother's picnic blanket was gripped under one arm. Georgia walked briskly through the night. This was exciting and strange. She couldn't remember being out by herself at night before. She made a bee line for the River.

The River had always fascinated Georgia in a way that she could not explain even to herself. It drew her. The notion of the River's power could only be felt, and even if you experienced it everyday it couldn't be explained. It seemed as though no one else shared the same regard for the River. And so even though thousands of people used the River and were near it, Georgia would get the impression that it was personal to her. She never learned anything new while being enchanted by her River; she would never tire of feeling that continuous volume of power.

Once close to the River, Georgia walked down North River Drive toward the park. She wouldn't be able to walk on the beach until she got past the small private properties. They were mostly small houses that were used as summer or vacation homes. She knew every house on this stretch of road. Georgia had probably walked down this road a thousand times. Darkness had turned the familiar surreal. Her Aunt Sarah's house was only about a block away. She wondered what Aunt Sarah would say if she saw Georgia out at that hour. This was very out of character for Miss Prim. Any of her relatives would probably *enjoy* hearing that Georgia did something as crazy as sneaking out to meet a man she hardly knew. It would be refreshing.

At last, the houses on her right gave way to open air. To her left, the park was looking very queer with only a few lights burning. She could barely make out the skyline of familiar shapes. The amusements had been shut down for over an hour. Groaning metal sounds came from workman adjusting something in the weird expanse of the park. Georgia felt unreal. The darkness was almost as weird as the silence.

The sky looked like it had been sprayed with stars. Was he here? Her thoughts leaped back to amazing Bobby. As soon as Georgia stepped into the sand she could see him. A figure in the distance. He was sitting with his hands casually around his knees at what would have been about a blocks distance away. She walked toward him. She had no real plans or expectations for this little rendezvous. Seeing him again didn't feel like an option. He rose and started toward her. Georgia enjoyed his walk. He looked more comfortable now than when she last saw him. Watching him walk toward her was satisfying enough. But he kept getting larger and larger until he was right there. He smiled that smile again. She was a gonner.

"Hello," Georgia meant to say it out load but it came out a whisper. She gestured with the picnic blanket to show him that she brought it. It was difficult to talk again. She felt so awkward.

"Hey, Peaches." He took her hand and they walked further up the bank. They spread the blanket out together and settled next to each other very naturally, like old friends. Georgia began to feel a little more relaxed. He seemed genuinely happy to see her and that helped. They settled in further and looked at the sky. He knew better than to try and pounce on her.

"Tell me about the city, I have never been," Georgia tried to sound casual.

"It's nothing compared to you," came his response. She realized there would be no casual chatter. She lay still and quite, forcing herself to become even more relaxed. As usual, Georgia's amazing self control proved successful. After a few deep breaths she was at ease. She wanted to enjoy her time with Bobby. Finally, she turned and faced him; her left arm was propped under her pretty head. Her right hand was on his chest.

"Why do I feel this way about you?," Georgia wondered out loud. She had just decided that the best thing to do was just to be as honest as possible.

"I've been asking myself the same thing," he answered. They laid there in silence for awhile. Being so close to Bobby felt great. She leaned over and pressed her right cheek on his left in a sort of embrace. She realized that she wanted to have sex with him. She asked herself if she was sure. Yup. Georgia didn't know how to proceed. She didn't know how to let him know. She unbuttoned the top of her blouse. That was all the invitation he needed. What followed could not possibly be put on paper without the risk of said paper igniting into flames.

About forty minutes later a smiling giggling Georgia wriggled back into her clothes. He was also getting dressed. This was the forth time she had ever had sex.

"You're not planning on leaving now are you?" he asked as he lay back down.

"Leave, are you kidding?! You're not getting rid of me that fast," Georgia answered as she settled in next to him. Being together seemed so important that neither one would have wanted to cut their night short. There really was no need for talking now.

The River lapped the beach. At that time neither one worried about how they would see each other again. It felt like being together was a given. As if they had been married for fifty years. Anyway, nothing mattered outside of those two; outside of that time. The air was so comfortable and they both felt so good being next to the other that they fell asleep.

# Chapter Five

Immediately Georgia was dreaming. It was a very intense detailed dream. The kind that you swear is really happening. Georgia was on a large expanse of countryside, surrounded by green hills as far as she could see. The skyline was huge. It was a pretty and peaceful countryside. The slope of the hillside was instantly familiar, as was the large fenced area to her left. She could have seen that homemade fence with her eyes closed. Off in the distance there was a small flock of sheep and a shaggy black and white dog. A man stood out there. Georgia's focus rested on the man. She was beginning to get annoyed because his supper was getting cold. Georgia whistled to him. As the man walked toward her she instantly recognized him. It was Bobby, and he was her husband. She couldn't tell how she recognized him because he looked different. He was much shorter. He had a square jaw, gorgeous smallish eyes, and thick brown hair. Handsome.

Suddenly two boys were running toward her from somewhere to the right of the little house that she was standing in front of. They looked to be about eight and six. When she saw their faces she remembered them as babies, and as toddlers. She remembered the songs she used to sing with the oldest and the time the youngest fell out of a tree. They were her sons. Her beloved boys. They kept running strait at her. The oldest crashed into her and wrapped his arms tight around her.

"I beat you! I won!," he shouted with his ear pressed to her chest. Georgia put her arms on him. The younger boy crashed into them and threw his arms around the pair. The boys started giggling, and Georgia did too. She looked up at the approaching man. He was wearing what looked to be homemade clothes, very plain and old fashioned. His face looked worn but he was strong and moved easily, he couldn't have been more than 30 years old.

"Hey, you hooligans get your mits off of my wife!" This only made the boys laugh harder. 'Bobby' embraced her and pressed his cheek to hers. They were the same height. She loved him intensely.

"Let's eat, I'm starved," the older boy declared. With her 'family', Georgia entered a very crude log cottage. The room she entered was large. There seemed to be a sitting area on her left and a kitchen on her right. The areas were only separated by a large long table. Once inside Georgia went strait to the stove. She found herself knowing where everything was. She ladled a simple soup out into four bowls. Each of her adoring men stood in line to accept a bowl. A basket of wonderful smelling sour dough bread was already on the big table. There were four earthenware mugs of water. The primitive table had two large benches on either side. Georgia took her seat next to her younger son, across from Bobby. This is where she always sat. She liked to have her back to the stove she that she could enjoy her meal without seeing the pot and utensils she had to clean up. In addition, in the winter time that side of the table was usually warmer. Her husband had declared very chivalrously that his wife and youngest would get to sit closer to the stove. At the current supper, nobody had yet lifted a spoon.

"Let us pray," Bobby began "Thank you, Lord, for this food that was excellently prepared by my beautiful wife, for the health that we enjoy, the success of our farm, and for our family and friends." Georgia peeked at Bobby now. His head was not bowed. He was looking at her with an intimate smile. She took his hand and they looked deeply at each other as he continued. "Lord, I am humbled for we are truly blessed by your amazing amazing grace."

"Amen."

\* \* \*   \* \* \*

Bobby looked at Georgia for awhile. He was stroking her hair as she slept. He enjoyed her softness. He stopped touching her hair and held her right hand with his left. Her head was on his chest and he turned his face into her hair as he closed his eyes. She was so precious to him. When Bobby fell asleep he found himself in another place and time. The dream felt real. He had just entered an extremely old-fashioned cottage. His hand was still on the wooden door handle. He looked around at the simple furniture, cooking area and fire. It was a large dimly lit room. The two windows were very small. Light calico fabric hung neatly around the windows. There was light from the fireplace on one side of the room, on the other side a little light came from the fire in the belly of a large black stove. In the center of this room there was a long wooden table with an oil lamp on it. The table had no chairs, it had a long bench on either side.

He felt short. His hands looked old and worn. A woman was there too. She was standing at the stove with her back to him. He recognized the rag she used to lift her tea pot off of the stove. She fixed two cups of something steamy and offered him one. He recognized the earthenware mugs that they used. He looked at that mug for a long time. He knew that he had been here before – been here for many many years.

He looked at the gray haired woman now and *remembered* her when she was young. She embraced him and pressed her cheek to his, her right hand was on the left side of his face. She smelled like soap. It was so familiar. This is what they always did. A wave of love and happiness swept up him. It felt like he hadn't seen her in ages and he had missed her desperately. But he didn't even know this 'wife' existed until just now. Leaning back from her Bobby realized she was Georgia, but she didn't look like Georgia. She looked a little surprised and pleased that he had held her especially close this time. She squeezed his arm in acknowledgement. She was the same height as he was. Her face was very mature but lovely. It was the way only a good woman could look. A woman who was loved dearly by her family, she had provided them with so much over the years. She was the soul of their family. To Bobby she was the most beautiful woman in the world.

This 'Georgia' moved past him now towards the fireplace. There were two simple wooden chairs facing the fire. On the chairs were cushions that looked homemade. Bobby waited for Georgia to sit and then sat in the opposite chair with his mug. The chair cushions had straw in them. Bobby looked at the fire place. It was a simple structure made of mostly large gray stones. The stones held special significance to him.

He remembered building that fireplace. He was barely a man when he married, and built her a house that was much wider than the one she grew up in. His father-in-law said he would have an awful time trying to heat the place. Hence the extra large fire place. They had had numerous special times in front of it. Romantic times alone together, then the excitement of babies on the way and newborns. He remembered the babies well now, only two boys. At the age of 22 she had fallen ill with a severe fever and never conceived again. He remembered the desperate prayers during her illness.

Then Bobby remembered the happy times. The fun of playing with the boys when they were small, holiday gatherings and birthdays, frequent friendly visits with family and neighbors –fits of laughter were not uncommon in this household. It all happened right in front of those stones very stones. They had been truly blessed. It was a joyous, harmonious household. These days their boys came to visit with their wives and little ones. Currently they had nine grandchildren with one more on the way. With the boys grown it was quieter now but still very happy. As Bobby sipped his tea he was sure that this house was the coziest place in existence. He smiled at his Georgia.

\* \* \* \* \* \*

The sun was now on his face. Bobby was back on that picnic blanket in the sand. He turned to look at the sleeping Georgia. A light breeze gently moved her hair. He ran his fingers down her bare arm. She opened her eyes and looked at him for about three seconds. Then she leaped up.

"I've got to get home!", Georgia straitened her skirt. She was quickly getting upset as she stumbled over her shoes and then frantically pulled them on. Her family might have woken up and realized she wasn't there! Georgia grabbed his hand and said goodbye quickly before rushing across the beach toward home.

"I'll see you in the park," she called back. Bobby said something she didn't understand. She just turned quickly and nodded. She was back to feeling awkward with him again.

She got home in record time and went around to the back door. By now Georgia realized it must be very early in the morning. She hadn't seen even one person as she sped home. She figured that all her neighbors were still in bed. She quietly opened the back door. Her mother was just entering the kitchen looking groggy. She jumped.

"Oh, Georgia you startled me!," she headed toward her coffee pot. Jean was in a light robe and night gown. "Why are you up and dressed this early?"

Georgia thought quickly.

"Mother, I've been up half the night with a terrible headache, I finally decided to go out and get some fresh air."

Georgia was not a good liar but her story seemed a heck of a lot more likely than, 'I spent the night on the River Beach with a criminal that I barely know'.

"Oh, Honey, can I fix you anything."

"No thanks, I think I'll go lie down upstairs."

## Chapter Six

Georgia had really only been pretending to be asleep for the past four hours. Everything felt wonderful. Having spent that time with him, and having *gotten away* with it! She was safe now. This time she had alone was almost as great as being with him. There was quite a bit to think about. At first she had been thinking about everything that happened on the River Beach with Bobby. Every move of it. How could she possibly think of anything else?! The early morning sun was on her back. She wrapped herself in her quilt and imagined being in his arms again. After she had exhausted those thoughts and practically given herself a fever, she moved on to thoughts of that vivid dream. The dream had such a peculiar setting. Georgia could understand why she might dream of being married to Bobby but she wondered why he looked so different.

It was obvious that she had a special bond with this man who was almost a stranger. She also knew that she could not be with him. Of course not, he was Italian, she wasn't even Catholic, not to mention his 'business', or the fact that everyone was so happy about her and Jacob. It would never work. Being a practical girl she told herself not to hold any thoughts that would encourage her feelings for Bobby. Instead she forced herself to remember why she loved Jacob. Why she knew she would say yes when she learned about the intended engagement. This took most of Georgia's self control but she was successful.

    She thought about the day that she first met Jacob. It was June of the previous year. A crew of four carpenters arrived early in the morning to get started on her Daddy's garage. The commotion outside woke Georgia up. She was attempting to enjoy sleeping in on one of her very first mornings as a high school graduate. Her annoyance turned to intrigue when she looked out the window. Through the swaying leaves and morning sunlight she caught a glimpse of her prince. He was strong and handsome in his sleeveless shirt. Georgia quickly located her most fetching outfit, dressed and hurried down stairs to watch them from the dining room window. She stood there trying to figure out why she might have reason to go out there and talk to them.

    Georgia had never been a girl that was crazy over boys, so when John and Jean figured out what was going on they knew this guy must be special. They really enjoyed catching Georgia at the window watching Jacob.

She was just far enough away from the window that she couldn't be seen from the outside. Georgia had one of the dining room chairs turned around so she could sit and gaze at this guy. After giving each other knowing looks Jean came up with an idea.

"Would you like to take out a pitcher of tea," Jean suggested.

"Oh, yes," Immediately her hand went up to her hair. I'll be right back. She ran to the bathroom. First, she carefully put on some makeup. She was finishing up on her hair when John called in,

"The poor guys are dying of thirst out there."

Georgia stepped out into the hall.

"How do I look?," She asked. Georgia was not the least bit embarrassed by how much her parents were enjoying this.

She did look beautiful.

"Too good if you ask me," came her Father's response.

"You look great Dear," said her Mother.

The pitcher of tea and four glasses were ready on the counter. Georgia had no trouble balancing it all. She took a breath and was out the door. She brought out the tea and spoke awkwardly for only a minute. Georgia returned to the back door with a triumphant smile. She had gone out there looking beautiful and that was enough -for that day anyway.

The next day Georgia baked cookies and just *couldn't imagine* what she was going to do with them all. Before she left to work at the park she dropped off a basketful to the workers outside. This time she was stunning, in a white sleeveless top, red skirt and matching red heeled shoes. She had to remove those shoes as soon as she got around the corner. But she could feel their eyes on her as she walked away. It was thrilling and a little embarrassing but it had to be done. The shoes gave her a swinging walk. Those painful shoes were worth every painful step. Georgia smiled now as she remembered that. She knew what she had to do in order to win her prince and she executed her plans perfectly. It was wit, cunning, and a pair of red heeled shoes that scored her one of the most desirable beaus in the county.

And so it continued that way, Georgia kept on finding a reason to stop and chat with Jacob. She always looked amazing and he was definitely interested in her. However, no matter how hard Georgia tried, Jacob would not ask her out. She did not understand matters such as professionalism. Jacob, having a very strong work ethic, did not think it was appropriate to pursue his client's daughter no matter how sweet and gorgeous she was. Certainly not while he was working. This whole matter frustrated both Georgia and Jacob. Georgia was close to her wits end when her Daddy helped her come up with a plan.

The next day was Sunday. John called the Layton's household in Woodstown and asked for Jacob. John asked Jacob for a favor. Doris and Georgia had gone to church that morning at the Friends Meeting House there in Woodstown. They had heard that the music was wonderful and have been bored with the services at our church. Anyway, he should have known better than to let them go alone because the silly things had run out of gas. Presently they were stranded at the Woodstown Diner and would he kindly go help them before they got into any more trouble.

So Jacob, happy to still be in his Sunday best, arrived at the Woodstown Diner minutes later. Only Doris wasn't there. Georgia sat alone at a table set for two complete with roses and sweet tea. She looked better than ever.

"Welcome to our first date, Mr. Jacob Layton."

Jacob stood there for a moment with his mouth agape.

"Your father thinks you're stranded here needing a ride home," Jacob was still confused.

"My *father* called you from the diner's phone and left me here when you said you were on your way," the beauty responded smoothly. Her makeup and hair was to die for. Olive had spent two full hours of her Saturday night setting Georgia's hair. Now Georgia sat with legs crossed, wearing a new skirt that was as short as she had ever dared to wear. She bounced her healed foot. With her seated the skirt revealed her knee. He couldn't help but notice what a fine knee it was.

Jacob laughed and smiled that smile she would come to love. He took his intended seat.

"Okay, our first date," he raised his tea glass,"to us."

"To us."

Jacob was the first real boyfriend Georgia had ever had. He took her out to a fine restaurant, and then to meet his parents. With him living all the way in Woodstown, it was a formal courtship. She saw him two or sometimes three times per week. They would talk on the phone almost every evening after dinner. They had spent a few dates in the park, and had spent some time with her friends and his. Jacob had three close friends, and they all thought Georgia was a good catch. They didn't hassle him too much about the time he spent with her.

Throughout the year they had spent a few special nights together in private. On those nights her parents thought they were out with a group of friends. Three times now they had parked. He didn't get too far that way. Three times they had retired to a vacant house belonging to one of Jacob's uncles. Jacob was supposed to keep an eye on the place occasionally when his uncle traveled.

They had had Sunday dinners at both his home and hers. Recently his parents were asking for her to come and spend more time in Woodstown. They wanted to 'get to know her better.' His family seemed to think fondly of Georgia.

\* \* \*   \* \* \*

Jean figured that noon was late enough. After all, the girl had to eat. She couldn't remember Georgia ever staying in bed all morning. By now Jean was thinking that her daughter must really be sick. She slipped into her room and set up a tray table with tomato soup and a cheese sandwich. Then she sat on the edge of the bed. Of course Jean didn't doubt her daughter's story at all. She placed a hand on Georgia's forehead. No fever. John was at work, and Olive had left with Shirley. Jean was beginning to like the idea of having Georgia all to herself for the afternoon.

Georgia pretended to wake up. Jean was smiling at her. Georgia looked like she was in a good mood. So Jean started right in.

"So, have you thought about what color dresses we should wear?

"Not yet," Georgia replied, stretching. "But I do know that I'd like to have drapes like Margaret's mother has for my dining room."

"Oh, it is a large dining room, isn't it? I can't wait to see it!" Jean said, "I don't recall the drapes at the Gant's house. What are they like?"

"They are rich and billowy in a red and green floral. Behind those she's got cream colored sheers."

"I think we can find a fabric like that, as soon as we get the measurements you and I will get started. Drapes are very easy to make," Jean was almost gushing like a girl.

"How about pale green for the dresses?," Georgia suggested.

"Green? I don't know," Jean thought about it.

"A very light green, like an Easter dress," Georgia explained.

"Well, it's going to be nearly fall by the time we get the wedding together. If we have it in August I guess we could do pale green dresses. In a very light weight material," Jean added.

"Everyone will use the same material but the dress will be made to suit each person. They will be a very simple style. Something that can be adjusted easily based on what neckline each person is comfortable with." Georgia hadn't given this much thought. What was coming off of the top of her head sounded pretty good. She must have heard this idea somewhere.

"Oh, that sounds great! I can picture the material now. Pale green will be lovely. It will look gorgeous with the flowers," Jean said, "how about mostly pink flower bouquets, with pink ribbons."

"Yes, that's what I was just thinking," Georgia was finally getting as excited as her mother was. "Pink and green is lovely together! Yes, that's it, Pink and green!"

"Well, we can't go get any material until after he gives you the ring," Jean said.

The ring! Georgia looked down at her left hand wondered about it.

The two women chattered on like that for most of the afternoon. At about 4 pm, Jacob called. He wanted Georgia to go to the drive in movie theater that Friday night, the movie started at 8:00.

"That sounds great, and don't forget the July Social at the dance hall is on Saturday night. You can still go right?," Georgia knew that he was very busy.

"Actually, I did forget. I am going to be pouring concrete Saturday and it is going to have to be finished that day. I'll make it there though. I'll meet you there," Jacob promised. So far, he had always kept his word.

"So I'll see you two days in a row this weekend. I can't wait!," Georgia said.

"Yea, I miss you, I love you," came Jacob's response.

Georgia felt a sharp stab in her heart. 'Why? Shouldn't she be happy now?,' she wondered to herself. 'Oh, yea, the criminal on the beach, it was only last night.'

"I love you too," Georgia managed.

"Do you have to work tomorrow?," Jacob asked.

"No but I have to work Friday, from 10:30 until 6:00."

"That's too many hours for you, Hun. No girl as pretty as you should have to work that many hours."

"Why I have no husband to support me. What's a girl to do?"

"I'll have to see what I can do about that," Jacob laughed. Georgia smiled. She loved hearing that he made her feel so safe, she loved his voice too.

"I love you. I have to say goodnight now, Olive is waiting to use the phone."

"Okay, I'll call you tomorrow. Goodnight, I love you, sleep good."

Georgia's emotions were in hyper over drive. It was the happiest most exciting time that she could remember but there was this stabbing guilt too. It was almost too much to bear. The next day was Thursday, the 4$^{th}$ of July. Georgia and Olive had thought to ask for this holiday off months ago. She was feeling overwhelmed so she was glad that she would be spending a day with her Mother and Sisters. Her Daddy would be off from work too. She was able to take comfort knowing that she would be surrounded by her immediate family.

## Chapter Seven

Jean woke Georgia and Olive early. There was baking to do, and cold foods to prepare. The corn bread muffins were already baking when the girls came into the kitchen.

"I've got something new we are going to try today," Jean announced. She opened the pantry cabinet and dug in the very back of it. Both Georgia and Olive realized their mother had been hiding something. Jean pulled something from the very back of the cabinet.

"It's prepared cake mix, Doris told me she used it for her sister-in-law's baby shower and the guests raved about her cake. It's supposed to be delicious. She was really tickled about it." Jean handed Georgia the small box so the girls could have a look. It was heavy for its size.

"Pillsbury prepared cake mix," Olive read aloud, "did anybody see you buy this?"

"Only that hundred year old clerk," Jean said, "I'm sure she didn't even know what it was."

It was a yellow cake. All they had to do was measure out a few ingredients and mix it all together. The box of cake mix even told them what temperature to bake at. The three where very interested in the recommended baking times depending on what size pan you baked your cake in. They tasted the batter and agreed it was wonderful. While that was baking they put together icing for the cake and a crust for the banana cream pie.

By 9 in the morning the three were hot and messy, but each item had turned out perfectly. Jean packed the corn bread muffins into the bottom of her large picnic basket. A riser inside of it would allow the banana cream pie to sit above the muffins. Jean loved showing off that basket. No one had been able to find one like it. The Spark's women were proud of their food. Next came their appearances.

After showering, Georgia and olive both chose sun dresses. Olive's sun hat was too big for her head but Georgia decided not to mention it.

"How do I look?," Olive asked her sister.

"Cute as can be. How about me?" Georgia asked twirling. She looked into their full length mirror. Georgia was almost embarrassed to go to a family party looking that good. She certainly didn't look like a kid anymore.

Jean was dressed beautifully too. She had the placement of those curlers down to a science. When she chose to do her hair it really turned out nice. Jean had on a pale blue light weight dress. The dress alone was unremarkable but her gorgeous blue sun hat and matching shoes were really enviable. At 11am John proudly escorted his three lovely ladies the block and a half to his family's picnic.

It was cooler than average on the forth of July that year and so the weather was comfortable at the Sparks family's annual picnic. John's sister Sarah hosted the gathering in her small riverfront back yard. Sarah was happy to be able to host something outside. She loved her home but it was too small to host a large indoor party. Sarah was a very small almost mousy woman. There was nothing remarkable about her appearance but she was always neat and respectable. Being a very savvy homemaker, Sarah was also always the first to have the new style of curtains, the latest recipe, or a fabulous idea for holiday decorating. Sarah was even the local expert on home fragrance as she was able to create the most long lasting potpourris. She hoped everyone would have occasion to pass through her home during the picnic. Sarah was especially proud of her home décor today.

Three long food tables were set up on Sarah's back porch. There was a magnificent array of food. A huge freight barge drifted past silently causing small waves on the river beach. Everyone enjoyed having the family picnic river side. The breeze was glorious.

Gabor, Doris, and the children arrived looking sharp. Gabor was carrying a large tray of deviled eggs. It hadn't been easy but Doris had managed to get everyone dressed impeccably *and* bring a decent dish. Jessie's dress was to die for. While Doris was greeting everyone, Jessie went after a balloon that was near the one patch of mud for a mile around. Doris gasped and darted after her daughter.

The disaster was narrowly avoided. It was answered by a boisterous laugh.

Doris looked around.

"I see Martha has graced us with her presence today," Doris said to the toddler.

"Oh, am I getting presents?!," Jessie squealed.

"You steer clear of that mud all day long, and I'll give you an extra special present when we get home. Sound good?"

"Yes, my Momma."

Doris wondered which piece of her costume jewelry she might have to sacrifice.

When Georgia was arranging small plates next to their cake she heard the word 'mansion' amidst a conversation. It had come from a clutch of Aunts and cousins, she rolled her eyes. Georgia didn't want anybody to know. It was supposed to be a secret for one thing. Secondly, she didn't need any help in the envy department. Martha would be in rare form, and Georgia still had to have word with her. For Olive's sake, of course. Georgia didn't care what her little confrontation would do to her relationship with her cousin. She already knew that she was one of Martha's favorite targets.

Her Aunt Irene's yelling interrupted Georgia's thoughts. Irene Sparks was the other nut on the family tree, so to speak. She was yelling at her husband, Bill, for not putting the hamburger buns in the basket *her* way. John's youngest brother, William, had married into money, a lot of money. They lived in the largest river front home in Lower Penns Neck. Unfortunately it was clear to everyone that all the money in the world didn't make up for Irene. Irene might have been forgiven for her controlling ways if she were dainty, or pretty, or was an excellent homemaker, or possessed some super interesting talent. The frumpy old yell bag had none of those things. At the moment, Irene was running her mouth and poor Bill's face was looking a little red. John's youngest sister, Elizabeth, a pretty petite forty something, stood with her back toward the scene.

"How, how, how could she possibly think that is appropriate?" Elizabeth said to Jean, Doris, and Georgia.

"Oh, there will be more Liz, just sit back and enjoy the show," Jean replied, although she didn't find Irene at all enjoyable. It really was not necessary for family to talk about Irene's behavior anymore; the subject was as old as the hills. Jean had never made the girls have sleepovers at Uncle Bill and Aunt Irene's even though they had children close in age. To tell you the truth all three of Jean's daughters had been afraid of Aunt Irene until recent years. The girls were not used to people speaking harshly. Jean and John's household was very harmonious, yelling was something that happened on rare occasion. In fact, in all their thirty three years together nobody had ever heard John or Jean disrespect the other.

While Olive was fixing a salad for herself she overheard someone say Georgia's name.

"Well, he's not certainly going to be a husband who will be able to spend time with her. The man is a slave to that company business," Martha said.

"Oh, I don't know about that Martha May," another cousin cut in.

"I do. Today is the perfect example. He's not here because he is working," Martha was proud of herself for making her point. "Georgia is in for a lonely life, if you ask me."

Olive wanted to ask Martha where *her* husband was, but being a lady she decided not to cause a scene.

Martha walked away from that group to greet an Aunt loudly. Obnoxiously.

Olive went off with her food to sit with Georgia. A group of men were having a great time playing bache balls. They were hollering and cheering. Georgia was laughing. Olive couldn't force herself to crack a smile.

"Something has got to be done about that witch," Olive began as she took a seat.

About an hour later Georgia had her opportunity. Martha was taking a look at the desserts, while Georgia sliced into the special yellow cake. Martha and Olive were the only people within earshot of her. Georgia would never lower herself to confronting someone publicly, even when that someone deserved it.

"Oh, Martha," Georgia began slowly, "maybe you could shed some light on something for me. Several of us have been wondering how a woman could grow to be 25 years old and not know that when you speak badly about other people you are only making yourself look bad." Martha's face got a little flushed. Georgia's insides got flushed, but it felt good. "I mean really, Martha, how could you not know? You embarrass yourself, Honey. You embarrass yourself quite a bit."

That stung, coming from her younger cousin who didn't say anything without good reason. It was unnecessary too, for Martha's sake anyway. Martha didn't need any help feeling bad about herself. Martha was miserable. Georgia realized this now but told herself that maybe she'd take it as advice. Maybe it would do her some good. Georgia looked at her little sister now, a slow smile spread across Olive's face.

"Well, we can't all be as good as Georgia Sparks now can we," Martha spat.

"No, *you* certainly never will be," Georgia replied cool as a cucumber. That last statement caused Olive to slap her hand over her mouth. Georgia knew it was cruel, but Olive's reaction was priceless.

"Well I never..," Martha began.

"You never what?," Olive chimed in. "You never are able to keep your jealous obnoxious mouth shut?" Her voice was a little shaky.

"*You* are a *disgrace* to this family, Martha May. You really should leave," Georgia spoke quietly. Mission accomplished. Nobody else heard a peep. Martha just stood there with her mouth wide open for a minute. Then she turned to get her tray of last-minute-pitiful-excuse-for cookies, and left. Olive thought she saw Martha's shoulders shaking as she walked toward the street with her head down. She must have been crying. Good. Maybe she learned something. The sisters didn't take too much pleasure in their little deed. They just tried to enjoy the day.

The wonderful breeze was moving ladies skirts and girls ribbons, it was carrying the happy music from the park to Sarah's yard. Laughter filled the air. Georgia and Olive decided to take Thomas and Jessie to play on the beach. All four of them removed their shoes at the edge of the grass. The sand was warm and felt good on their feet.

"Aunt Olive, can *I* wear it?," Jessie asked.

"Wear what, Honey?"

"Your big hat," Jessie pointed at it.

"Yes you may. Be careful with it." Olive put the enormous hat on her head.

Thomas was busy already drawing with a long stick in the sand. Jessie ran toward him.

"Look Brother, my hat."

She fell forward in the sand. She stood, looked down at herself, and started to cry. Thomas got to her first.

"I'm a bad girl," she wailed, although she obviously wasn't hurt.

"No Sister, you're not a bad girl. Only a bad thing happened," Thomas had his little hand on her little back.

Georgia and Olive thought this little exchange was so cute that they didn't interfere.

"Look, I can fix it ." Thomas brushed the dry sand off of Jessie's dress. "All gone," he said.

"All better," Jessie sniffed.

"Oohh," Olive cooed to Georgia.

Georgia giggled and said, "They are so darn cute."

\* \* \*   \* \* \*

"Jean this cake is wonderful. I've never had anything like it," Irene said as she approached Jean.

"Would you believe that I got that recipe from Doris? I think we are going to keep it a family secret."

"Well it is a delicious secret. I'll be asking you to bring this to my next party," Irene kept on walking, and Jean was glad.

Jean and Elizabeth had kept themselves amused for the afternoon by counting how many times Irene hen pecked Bill. It was so unlike Jean, but by the end of the picnic the two ladies where almost crying in hysterics over it. There laughter together was so genuine that caught the men's attention and made the young ladies a little jealous. For a moment there, without intention, Jean and Elizabeth were once again the most attractive women in Lower Penns Neck. It was something in there voices and in their posture.

The ladies all helped to pack up the remaining food, and clean up. The men folded up tables and chairs. Jean had had a really good time and was smiling as she carried her special basket home. Her daughters seemed satisfied too.

Once back on Cherry Street not long after they arrived home Jacob called. While Georgia was on the phone Jean was putting the large basket away in the bottom of her hutch. Georgia overheard her mother mutter to herself, "I wonder where my picnic blanket has gotten to?"

Jean was in an especially good mood and did not seem overly concerned, but this hit Georgia like a ton of bricks. It was as if meeting with Bobby was only in her head until now. Now she grasped that it was real. There, while on the phone with her adoring boyfriend, Georgia was crushed by the gravity of it.

Jacob could tell that something was wrong. He thought she was upset that he wasn't able to come to her family's picnic.

"Oh, no it's not that. I just suddenly don't feel well. I may have eaten something bad."

"Georgia, I wish I could be there to take care of you."

His sweetness only made it worse. Her head swam.

"I think I should get ready for bed now. Thank you for calling, I'll see you tomorrow okay?" Georgia's voice cracked a little.

"Okay, but I don't want you going to work tomorrow if you're sick. Do you hear me, Hun?"

"Yes, I love you. Goodnight."

"I love you, too. Goodnight."

Olive fell asleep quickly that night, leaving Georgia alone with her thoughts. Clearly it was *her* who was a disgrace to the family. Would she be a bad person for the rest of her life? A bad person! She buried her face in her pillow and sobbed quietly. Mostly she cried because she was sure that Jacob deserved a trustworthy wife. Georgia didn't get much sleep that night.

## Chapter Eight

Bobby had his regular business in the park that day but that was second to making sure he got to talk to Georgia. Bobby couldn't get that dream out of his head. He now remembered many details from what he had begun to think of as his 'past life.' He remembered the immediate area around the house he had dreamt about. There was the lean-to room he finally added after twenty years of his wife's pestering. In addition there were these two men whom he recalled quite a bit about. He knew them as children and as adults. Could they be his sons? Was it really what it seemed to be? Could he really have been married to Georgia in a different time and place? It seemed obviously so, but at the same time so bazaar. He did not know how to handle the situation and was becoming desperate for answers. He was desperate enough to want to spend another night on the beach. He knew he'd be stranded there until the next day and he wasn't even sure if she would show. This thing with Georgia was starting to take over his life.

Bobby was in the park before he realized he had taken an earlier ferry today. He was so anxious to see Georgia. His gut feeling was just to take her. Just to take her by the arm and take her back to the city. However,

Bobby knew that he had to maintain control over any impulsive actions that might make her run away. He was not used to having such strong feelings for a woman.

* * *   * * *

  Georgia felt loathsome when she woke up. She figured work would help her to earn back a little bit of self respect. It was difficult to act cheerful with her family before she left home. She was glad that Olive wasn't working and she could walk alone. She didn't have to pretend to feel normal. She could just disappear into that strange crowd. That strange joyous crowd. Thousands of people that had no earthly business in this rural county. Even so close to home Georgia felt like she could hide out in that crowd. She was doing exactly what she was supposed to be doing and she owed nobody an explanation for the serious expression on her young face.

  Not only did Georgia feel horrible about going behind Jacob's back with another man, but she was starting to not know how she would ever say goodbye to Bobby. She couldn't begin to figure out how to resist him. Even if she could somehow resist him, the thought of not seeing him again was unbearable. In the park a country recording was playing. Above the fiddle Hank Snow sang:

  *You've switched your engine now I ain't got time*
  *For a triflin' woman on my main line*
  *'Cause I'm moving on*

*You've done your Daddy wrong*
*I've warned you twice now you can settle the price*
*'Cause I'm moving on*

'That's what Hank Snow would think of me.' Georgia thought. 'I am a triflin' woman.'

She made it to her booth on time, tied on her apron, and began getting things organized. Keeping busy was a small relief. As she worked that morning in her tired emotional state she thought to herself that maybe Bobby was all in her head. Nobody else had seen him. Maybe it was just a silly fantasy and it would all go away. She concentrated on the band music playing nearby. She allowed herself to be soothed by it. She imagined lyrics were there wasn't any. 'It's just a silly dream,' she made the horns say in her mind. 'Just a silly dream.' 'Everything will be fine,' the sax cut in, 'just fine.'

No such luck. There he was. He had no jacket on today, his eyes looked more intense than usual. He looked good. Her head started swimming with thoughts of their time on the beach. Nobody else knew about this situation. Nobody could help but him. She wanted so badly to be in his arms. He just sat there. This intense desire just to bury her face in his chest rendered her speechless as she made him his regular sandwich. Her hands shook. Bobby was not affected by Georgia's silence. After some uncomfortable small talk he said, "I really need to see you again, even if it's just one last time."

"I don't -I don't know," Georgia managed without looking at him.

"I have to see you. I'm staying on the beach tonight," he concluded, "I'll be waiting for you." The shock of those words made her look at his face. He still had that effect on her.

He left her with a wink and an extra twenty dollar bill. He really did need to attend to his business or else he would have stayed longer. He had seen enough longing in her face that he was confidant that she would be back to see him. Feeling this Bobby was happy as he walked away.

She wanted to yell for him to come back. She wanted to climb into his shirt pocket and live there forever. This was by far the most complicated and emotionally confusing situation that Georgia had yet faced. And it had just gotten worse. She just stood there swaying. A feather might have knocked her down.

'Triflin'.'

Many people stopped for tea and lemonade that day. Georgia had to walk with a wagon to refill her pitchers three times. There was very few customers for sandwiches which she had come to expect on hot days like this. At the end of the workday Georgia decided she would do a little shopping. She desperately needed to do something happy and normal. There was a boutique on Broadway. The prices were reasonable. Bobby's twenty dollar bill would buy a new outfit for that night and a dress for the July Social.

She remembered the times she walked to the boutique with her mother and sisters as a child. Georgia had had a wonderful childhood, mostly because of her mother. Those were carefree times. She wanted that back. Broadway and the shops only looked slightly different than they had been when Georgia was little. She tried hard to recreate the feeling of 'going to the boutique' from her childhood. The same old hanging bell rang as she pushed open the door. The music from the park was faint now. Georgia saw an outfit featured on one of the two dressing dolls. It was a stylish pair of claim digger pants and a close fitting top. It was different and smart looking.

She had been refusing to wear pants even though both of her sisters had owned a couple of pairs. She insisted that she didn't like them when she was twelve and never really cared to own a pair since. These would be her first. They caught Georgia's eye because she thought the cut would be flattering on her. Once she found her size in the pants and featured top she took them to the small dressing room. The outfit looked excellent. The top was a very lightweight burgundy colored material and sleeveless. The pants were short, the hem was at her mid calf. They were awfully flattering. She stepped outside the dressing room so she could stand back from the mirror to get a better look. Wow. She wanted to kick herself for never wearing pants before.

"Look at you," came a friendly voice. It was the boutique owner, Beatrix. She was a high school friend of Jean's. "My Goodness, Dearie. Would you like to model my clothes?"

"I'll tell everybody where I got these!" Georgia gushed. Forcing herself to be sweet and sociable truly helped to brighten her mood. Suddenly she was not as tired. This stop had been just the thing.

"That's a good girl."

"I'll take both of these. And would you help me choose a dress for the July social? The same size."

Beatrix returned with two floral knee length full skirt dresses, and one fitted gray dress with black trim.

"Thank you. I'll try the gray one first." Georgia said excitedly. Then she eyed the other two more closely. She wanted to remind Beatrix that she was *nineteen* now, but she let it go. "Oh, Beatrix, this is wonderful! Do you have a hat that matches?"

"I sure do. My, they must be paying pretty well in the park these days." Beatrix said as she admired Georgia in the dress and reached for the hat.

"I have been getting some good tips lately." Georgia said absently as she placed the matching hat over her lovely brunette mane.

"Georgia Anne Sparks you are an absolute vision!," Beatrix announced.

"Ooh, I'll take it! I'll take all four pieces! And I will tell everyone where I have been shopping." Georgia stepped back into the dressing room. "I have black shoes that will be excellent with this dress! I have a date tonight with Jacob and I just can't wait to see his face when he sees me in pants!"

Georgia dressed quickly and waited as Beatrix rung up her bill. "These are my first pair of pants."

"They are a very nice pair, and from a good maker too. Wash those in cold water only and they should last you a good long time. Twelve eighty."

Georgia paid, thanked Beatrix and was out the door. Beatrix wondered what it would be like to just throw on something new and look gorgeous.

Clothing was usually bought only one piece at a time, so it had been a big shopping trip. As Georgia walked home on Broadway she only hoped she would have time to lie down before she needed to dress for her date with Jacob. Georgia came in the front door.

"Hello, Hun, how was your day?" Came Jean's voice. "Oh a shopping bag, let me see." Jean set down her iron and came over to have a look.

"You'll never guess what I got." Georgia said. She set her large bag down on the sofa and lifted out the pants. She was glad to have come in with a distraction, it helped hide that there was something wrong with her.

"I knew you'd get a pair eventually. Honey, these are nice.," Jean cooed. Olive was instantly in the living room ready to inspect the purchases. She must have heard the bag rustling. It was like cat nip. Georgia lifted out the dress next.

"Wow, you must have spent a fortune!," Olive gasped as she peeped into the tall bag. "Can I borrow this hat?," it was already on her head.

"I made twenty one eighty in tips today!," Georgia announced.

"What! Over twenty dollars! Holy Cow Georgia!" Olive laughed.

"My goodness," Jean was dumbfounded.

"And yes, you may borrow the hat *after* I wear it to the July social tomorrow night."

"Well then can I wear your white dress with the blue sash?," Olive asked. Up until this afternoon it was the best piece of clothing Georgia owned.

"Yes you may."

Olive hugged her sister. "Oh wow! Next year I am definitely going to work in a sandwich booth! Over twenty dollars in one day, I can't believe it!"

"Wait 'till I tell your father," Jean said as she happily went back to her ironing. Georgia went upstairs to hang up her new clothes.

There was no time to lie down. Jacob called and said that he'd be there at four. She only had a half an hour. He said he wanted to show her something in Woodstown, they would have dinner and then be at the drive in theater for 'The Street Car Named Desire' which would start at seven.

Jean overheard the conversation.

"This could be it, Honey, he could be asking you tonight!" Jean had her hands clasped together. Georgia felt a wave of excitement. She looked at her bare left hand, raised her beautiful brows and then dashed to the bathroom for a shower.

Thirty minutes later, Jacob was in the Sparks's living room chatting with John and Gloria. Georgia came down the steps slowly, purposefully making an entrance.

"Well, look at you," Jacob said, clearly impressed. She looked more stylish than he had ever seen her. "You look beautiful."

"And she's rich too," John cut in. "Tell him about your tips today." Jacob and Georgia embraced respectfully. Jacob looked great. She kissed him sweetly on the cheek.

"I made twenty one eighty in tips today!," her eyes were intent on Jacob's face. She had missed him.

"Hey, no kidding?!," Jacob gaped. "That's amazing!" He turned to her parents and said, "this girl has been working too hard!"

"Well it was mostly one really large tip." Georgia said.

Jacob was interested but said, "We'd better get going. I'll have her back by ten."

"Sharp!," said John and then he chucked. He knew Georgia was in good hands.

"You have a good evening," came Jacob's reply.

"Have a great time, Honey," Jean embraced her daughter and gave her a wink.

"We will, Mother," Georgia said smiling.

Outside Jacob opened the passenger side door. The truck had been thoroughly cleaned. 'Maybe tonight is the night,' Georgia thought. Once Jacob was seated he leaned in for a proper greeting. They shared a long kiss, his left hand was on her face.

"I missed you," he said.

"I missed you," she said, and then embraced him fully. She pressed her face into his neck. He was so comforting. She held on as long as he would let her. Georgia felt comforted and dizzy at the same time.

"So one really large tip, huh, that must be an interesting story." Jacob started the truck, and they were off.

'Oh, no I shouldn't have said that!,' Georgia thought to herself. A stab in the chest and now a tightness in her throat. She was not used to having a secret to keep. Her mind raced, 'Is Jacob really asking me something about Bobby! *That* Bobby, the one I had S-E-X with?! Say something QUICK!'

"Some old rich guy from Philadelphia, he had his little girl with him. He looked very old to have a 7-year-old daughter." ('Holy cow, where did that come from!?')

She faced out the passenger side window as she spoke. "He left me a twenty dollar bill!"

"You know how those rich city guys are, his wife is libel to be twenty years younger than he is. I guess it was your lucky day, huh?" Jacob was smiling. The danger seemed to be passed but that did not end Georgia's panic attack.

"Yea, and the money was just the beginning." Georgia laced her fingers with his. "So where are we going first?" Her heart was racing.

"I am taking you to see my work site. It is close to were we will be having dinner and we have accomplished a lot since the last time I showed it to you," Jacob was happy, thus far he was oblivious to her panic.

"Oh, that sounds lovely, Jacob, I was interested in seeing it."

"I am very proud of it. It's a real beauty."

"Will we be going to the Woodstown Diner?"

"You guessed it."

Of course the diner is where they had their first date. Georgia was thinking that either of these places could be where he planned to propose. She was excited to see the house. This did not help the heart racing. She just hung on to his hand for the rest of the ride taking slow breaths; there was nothing else she could do.

Once on Main Street, Georgia eyed the gorgeous old Victorian style homes. They had been preserved well and were interesting. These would be her neighbors. There were not many homes like this in Lower Penns Neck. They pulled up to the giant white Victorian style house. It was made to match the old houses on Main Street. This house was larger and set back from the street on a larger yard. The exterior looked almost complete. It was twice the width of her parent's generous home, with a full second story and probably a walk up attic above that. There were large screened sunrooms flanking each side of the house. A stately portico framed the lavishly detailed front door. There were many large windows. Black shutters had been hung on the first floor windows.

"Jacob it's gorgeous!," Georgia declared as he opened her car door. She hopped out like a little kid. He was a surprised by her excitement.

"Would you like to see the inside?"

"Oh, could we?"

"Yes," he laughed now at how excited she was, "but you'll have to watch your step, and stay close to me it is still a construction site."

Georgia tried to get a hold of herself. She didn't want Jacob to know that her Daddy had spoiled the surprise. She took deep breaths as they approached and he took a moment to unlock the door. Across the street there was a row of smaller historic looking well kept homes. Each house had its own personality. It was a charming neighborhood. Large trees shaded the sidewalk and lawns. Georgia had to try hard not to hop up and down.

The front door opened into a grand foyer. The woodwork on the stairs was exquisite. She walked in and put her hand on the banister.

"Did you do this?," Georgia asked quietly. She was in awe now.

"No, I can't take credit for the banister we hired out for that. I did do the crown moldings and the woodwork on the archways and windows. And this." He led her strait back to a swinging door. He wanted to show her how it swung both ways. "There are two of these doors on the kitchen one here, and one leading to the dining room. It keeps the heat in and it's easy to open when you are carrying a try of food." Jacob demonstrated by walking backwards through the door. It swung open easily.

"Wow, you guys are brilliant! Really brilliant, this is amazing!" Georgia stepped into the kitchen. It was as big as Aunt Irene's, maybe bigger! A window above the sink looked out over a picturesque back yard. There looked to be about a half an acre behind the house. There were a few large trees. Saint Joseph's church and graveyard was visible beyond the property. The countertops were not on yet but the cabinets were up and they were exquisite. Dark cherry wood. The most beautiful she had ever seen. Her hand was on her mouth now. She knew she didn't deserve those cabinets. How could *she*, the women who snuck behind his back in the worst way, deserve this? She didn't talk much for the remainder of the tour. She asked a few appropriate questions and told him she was impressed. Jacob seemed content with having shown her the house. However, by this point he noticed that Georgia was acting strange. She was distant.

She was overwhelmed to the point of almost losing it. There were these stabbing pains in her throat and chest. She wondered why she kept trying to figure out how long it would be before she could sneak out to the beach. 'Am I really planning on seeing him tonight? Why? Because I can't resist him. Because I can't stand the thought of him waiting for me without going to see him.'

She just started to shut down in self defense. She went through the motions.

It was a very short drive to the Woodstown Diner. While Jacob spoke briefly to the hostess, Georgia must have caught the eye of the owner of the diner. Jacob saw him pretending not to be watching her. On the way to their table Jacob caught another man who was impressed by his girl. Jacob put his hand on her waist and tried to make eye contact with the guy. It took the stranger a moment to realize that the young man escorting the beauty was staring him down. Georgia was unaware of the attention she was getting. Jacob briefly introduced Georgia to two couples that he knew and one of the carpenters that he worked with. After they sat, Jacob just admired her for awhile. He felt especially lucky to have her.

Jacob ended up ordering for Georgia because she looked like she would never decide what she wanted to eat. They spoke pleasantly about nothing in particular. She had to force herself to pay attention to him. He asked her at least three times if she was feeling alright. Jacob decided she was defiantly working too much and he would have to put a stop to it, but not tonight. That discussion could wait. It took a long time for their dinner to arrive. Jacob joked that the plump waitress had made off with their meals.

"Jacob, you are so bad," Georgia exclaimed but she giggled anyway. Through the meal she managed to throw him loving glances and he seemed only slightly unhappy with her performance.

*A Streetcar Named Desire* was premiering that night at the Drive-in Movie Theater on Route 40 in Carney's Point. Because it was the first showing of the film in their area Jacob had paid a 60 cents per ticket. That was full 10 cents more than regular price. He had grumbled about the cost when he purchased the tickets but nothing was too much for his Georgia. He thought this film would be a special treat for her. On their second date she had talked about how much she enjoyed the play. They where really getting to know each other at that time she told him how much she had been impressed by her first trip to a theater. It really was a special time for her. It was more the atmosphere of the large theater that she enjoyed rather than the show itself.

Once in the car on their way to the theater, Jacob realized that Georgia hadn't bothered to ask what film they would be seeing.

"Aren't you curious to know what film we are seeing?"

Georgia thought quickly, she really was an actress tonight.

"Why, I am just so thrilled to be going out with the best catch in the county, I'm not sure it matters what film I see." She flashed him a winning smile that made him not care in the least what the girl bothered to do or not do.

"It's *A Streetcar named Desire*. I remembered how much seeing the show meant to you."

"Oh," she was disarmed, "I was interested in seeing that, thank you." Georgia squeezed his hand. Could this man be any more perfect for her.

They arrived at the theater early enough to secure a decent spot. Georgia wished the film would start already. Jacob wouldn't stop staring at her. She needed to pretend to be into the film so that she could hide.

"My Lord in Heaven you are gorgeous in this light" Jacob whispered. She gave an uncomfortable smile, and allowed him to kiss her.

Finally the film was playing. It was not exactly like the play, it had been censored to be less controversial. For awhile Georgia was soothed by losing herself in the story. However her comfort was short lived, the more she watched the pretentious main character, Blanch, the more she questioned her own virtue. Blanch was a ridiculous woman who was losing her mind. She pretended to be a fine virtuous woman but in reality she was scandalous to the extreme. 'Am I any better than her?! Am I losing my mind?!'

   Jacob was not interested in the movie. She had to accommodate him. She had come up with only one way to kiss him the way he needed her too. That was to think about Bobby. This went on for several minutes. She was making him happy, but she had to imagine Bobby. 'Slut,' Georgia actually called herself this in her mind. It hurt a lot. She choked back a sob.

"What's wrong?"

"I'm sorry. I think I might still be a little sick. My stomach just isn't right."

Jacob was considering proposing tonight. He wasn't sure when or where. He had practiced what he would say. His plan beyond that had only been to wait until the time felt right. It was starting to seem like the time would never be right.

"Can I get you anything? Maybe a soda?," Jacob was genuinely concerned. Georgia enjoyed his patience and the fact that he wanted to take care of her.

"Yes, a soda would be great, thank you."

"Okay, I'll be right back." He looked at Georgia before he walked away. He looked happy, she could see that he really adored her. Once alone she curled to her right and laid her head on the passenger door, eyes closed.

Jacob appeared to have cooled off after his trip for the soda. He didn't keep trying to kiss her, maybe he was considering her supposed stomach ache.

It was well after nine when they headed back to Lower Penns Neck. She gripped his hand tightly as he drove. Her heart wouldn't stop racing. Georgia leaned her head back, and wondered quietly if this is what it felt like to really lose it. She was shutting down.

'How could I have done it?! What am I going to do? I can't see Bobby again! I'll never look into those eyes or feel him touch me again?!,' her eyes started to fill up behind her pretty closed lids.

After they pulled up to the Spark's home, Jacob put his arms around Georgia and held her for awhile. Georgia's thoughts went back to the proposal. 'This could be it!' They shared a tender farewell. He said he hoped she would feel better soon. She thanked him for a lovely evening and kissed him as best as she could.

Jean was sitting backwards on the couch so she could look out the window. Georgia opened the front door. Her mother almost fell backwards when she hopped up from the couch. John just chuckled.

"So?" Jean gushed. "Lets see it!"

"No ring yet. But we had a nice evening and he took me to see the house." Georgia figured she needed to start calling it the 'house' rather than the 'mansion'. She didn't want to seem pretentious. Jean was disappointed, but she settled for a thorough description of the large house. John smiled from his comfortable chair as he watched Georgia thrill her mother with details about her future home.

    Olive was actually asleep when Georgia entered their bedroom. She was still half dressed and had a book on her chest. Georgia lay down in bed without changing her clothes. She was desperately hoping to quiet her racing mind. Unfortunately the opposite occurred. Without any distraction she became more and more stressed. She lay completely still for a good hour.

# Chapter Nine

She needed to talk to someone. There was nobody she could say these things to but Bobby. Besides, maybe just spending a little time with him would help her sort things out. Georgia decided she would be sneaking off to the beach, but only for a little while. First she stood outside of her parent's bedroom door expecting to hear something. Surprisingly she determined that they had already dropped off to sleep. Once again the girl slipped silently through the house and out the back door.

The night air was a nice change from the stifling bedroom where she had been agonizing. The sky held a few thin clouds. The moon and stars were remarkable. Surreal. Georgia ran. Her healed feet slapped the ground. She hated herself for the excitement growing in her chest. Once on the beach she removed her shoes and, clutching them, ran barefoot through the sand. Her feet threw up sand behind her.

He was there. Bobby was reclining in the same spot where they had spent the night only three nights before. He didn't notice her until she was fairly close. She dropped to her knees near her Bobby. He had a bottle of wine and two large wineglasses. His eyes were watery. Bobby reached for her hand. He was so gorgeous that she was humbled. He needed her. Her heart overflowed. In a second she was in his arms. With her face pressed into his chest she let go of her pain in heaving sobs.

"I was starting to think you weren't coming," Bobby whispered into her hair. She could feel how relieved and happy he was. He didn't seem to be bothered by her crying. She wailed like a little kid. It was several minutes before she could speak.

"Oh my God, I missed you," she breathed into his neck. Georgia kissed him passionately. She climbed onto his lap and sat. He was leaning on a sand bank with a couple of beach towels beneath him. He eyed beautiful Georgia as he carefully filled both glasses to the top. Bobby was enormously pleased.

"You look great, Peaches"

"So do you."

She alternated between leaning in for gentle kisses and sipping her wine. It was amazing. Just being together fulfilled them both. This was Georgia's third alcoholic drink ever and she hadn't eaten much that day. They enjoyed looking at each other and touched affectionately. He filled her glass a second time. It wasn't long before she needed to lie down next to Bobby. Her glass ended up in the sand and her head on his chest. He smelled so good; she wanted to live there forever. And maybe she would. In the world, in the universe, weren't they together? Wouldn't they always be together? Georgia had a long period of trying to hang onto that moment. She would be able to revisit it for life. His breathing rocked her gently up and down. Up and down. The stars became blurry and she dozed off.

*   *   *     *   *   *

Georgia sat strait up. She was no longer on the beach. She was in a bed that sat high off of the floor. She had been covered by a multicolor quilt. She looked down at the quilt that now covered her legs and belly. A man was next to her in bed. He was slowly arousing from sleep. It was a decent sized bed room. Everything in the room was beyond old fashioned, it was almost primitive. This could be the cottage she had dreamed of before. There was a small fireplace near her side of the bed. The furniture was simple but large. An oil lamp shown yellow from the top of the dresser. From the small window she could see that it was day, but a quite stormy day. There was a tree branch tossing around not far outside that little window. She recalled agonizing over getting those little curtains just right. Thunder rumbled. Rain tapped the window. It was the perfect day for an afternoon nap. Georgia's belly touched the top of her leg. Her belly felt hard. She saw that she was pregnant. Weird.

The man had his eyes opened now and was smiling gently at her. It was Bobby, it was the 'other' him that she had dreamt of before. He looked different this time, younger. He may have even been a teenager. Bobby's hair was a thick tosseled brown mess. His eyes were light brown, he had a boyish smile.

"Georgia?," he whispered so soft she almost didn't hear him, "is it you?"

"Yes, …Bobby? Where are we?" It seemed like a ridiculous question because this felt like the most familiar place in the world.

"In *our* house. In *our* house, in another time and place. When we were married," Bobby spoke a little louder now. His hand was on her back.

"I was in this place before, when we slept on the River Beach before."

"So was I."

Georgia spoke slowly now, "I remember this place – and you -and our sons –and our *life*."

"Me too. I can't get it out of my head." Then taking her hand he said, "Please lay down, let's be together, I just want to be next to you." Georgia was overwhelmed. She did lie down on her side facing him, but she squeezed her eyes shut. She wanted to get out of there.

"I can't handle this, I want to go home," She whined. Bobby started stroking her hair to comfort her.

"Come here." He turned and got his shoulder under her head. He held her and she did start to feel better. The stress was fading away. The quilt and mattress were so comfortable. Lightning flashed and then there was a far off rumble. She wondered what she had been stressed about. Her life as Georgia was fading from her mind. No. This was not okay. She received a startling baby kick in her belly.

"No!"

Black night again. Somebody's forgotten beach towel was crumpled behind her. He had awoken too.

"I want to go." Georgia was almost crying again.

"Peaches wait," he said softly. She yanked her arms from him.

"No, I'm sorry. I'm so sorry. I have to go." She was crying now.

What could he do? He watched the girl go. It was painful but at least he felt closer to the truth.

Georgia ran for home. She had her sobs under control by the time she reached the edge of the park. She stopped for a minute and took a breath. All she could think about was getting into her bed, into her room -where she belonged.

Georgia had to give herself a pep talk. "In a few minutes, I will be safe at home. I am going to enjoy my engagement and wedding, and I'll *never* do anything wrong again!" At that moment Georgia was so stressed by the incident that she couldn't wait to get started on the 'never doing anything wrong again.' She needed to earn Jacob. She had to. Feeling guilty for the rest of her life was not an option. Her feet pounded the street. She let her emotions power through her legs and pound the street. It must have been very late. There wasn't a soul in sight.

Just the sight of home was a relief. She entered the house silently and climbed the stairs. The light was on in their room. Georgia was still out of breath.

"Where were you? I've been worried sick! I almost woke up Mother and Daddy!," Olive said in a harsh whisper.

"Oh," Georgia fell face first into bed. Olive stared at her incredulously for a minute, then came over to sit next to her.

"What's going on? Are you okay?," Olive's voice was only concerned now.

"No," Georgia turned her head into her pillow and was crying once again.

"I was out with another guy," came Georgia's muffled voice. She figured she might as well just get it out. Wow, she said it. It actually feld good. Georgia let out a deep breath.

Olive said nothing, she just covered her mouth. Georgia was still lying face down. She turned her face from the pillow so she could explain.

"He's been coming to my sandwich booth. And there has been just something about him and I just couldn't resist him!," Georgia cried. "I spent the night on the beach with him on Tuesday!"

Olive sucked in her breath. Neither spoke for a few minutes. Georgia was crying into her pillow. Then Olive asked, "You're not going to see him again are you?"

"No, no," Georgia sobbed.

"So that's what's been wrong with you!"

"Yes," Georgia was a little more relieved. For once she felt like the little sister. She had taken care of Olive enough times, Olive could take care of her this once.

"It's totally over; you're not going to see him again?" Olive asked again.

"No! I don't want this to have happened in the first place. I am a bad person forever now!," She put her face back in the pillow.

Georgia lay there silently now she had caught her breath; she was relieved to have Olive to help her through this. Georgia wondered what Olive was thinking. Had she let down her little sister? Olive had a hundred questions on her tongue, but was quiet for a long time. She just rubbed Georgia's back.

"No Sister," Olive finally spoke slowly. "You're not a bad girl. Just a bad thing happened."

Georgia sucked in her breath, turned and looked at Olive solemnly for a full twenty seconds. Then they both giggled nervously. Georgia took Olives hand.

"I am so sorry. Please, never tell anybody, promise?," Georgia looked serious again.

"Promise."

## Chapter Ten

Georgia slept in very late. Olive was wearing the white dress with the blue sash when Georgia opened her eyes. It all came rushing back. 'Oh my Lord, Bobby! I told her about Bobby!' Georgia's hand went up to her forehead, and she stared at her sister. Olive did not seem phased by the devastating news.

"How should I wear my hair?," Olive had both of her hands in her hair. Georgia sat up.

"Very curly, I'll help you set it," Georgia felt better after getting so much sleep.

"You will help me with mine, won't you."

"Yes, and I've already spoken to Shirley and Margaret. They will be here at two with their dresses. I thought it would be fun for us all to get gussied up together!"

"That sounds great," Georgia got out of bed and stretched. "I need to get something to eat."

"Breakfast was cleaned up three hours ago," Olive said while looking in the mirror. The dress looked better than Georgia remembered it.

As Georgia stared across the room to get her robe Olive stopped her. She held her big sister by both arms and looked at her seriously. "I've been thinking a lot about your little incident. I want you to know that it's okay. I love you and you deserve to be happy. If it is really over with this guy than you need to just move on and forget about it. Don't beat yourself up. Do you understand?"

"Yes." Georgia smiled and she felt as if something heavy had just peeled off of her. "Thank you." Georgia couldn't remember ever loving her sister as much as she did right then.

Margaret arrived first carrying her dress on a hanger, in her other arm she had a case containing hair rollers and make up. The rollers were not for her. Margaret's reddish hair was curly enough.

"Hello all," she called as Jean opened the door for her. "I brought Bernicie's rollers and every bit of makeup I could find. Let's see your dresses."

Georgia was coming down the stairs trying not to look like she just woke up. Margaret was short, she was also the heaviest girl of the click. She had strong legs and shoulders, very cute.

"Let's get our hair set first and then have some lunch," Georgia suggested.

Minutes later the three girls were in the upstairs bedroom. Margaret set Georgia's hair while Georgia set Olive's. It was a beautiful sunny day. Georgia was glad for the company.

"Grandmom told me an interesting story last night," Olive began.

"What about?," Georgia was so not interested and hoped Olive would not be boring Margaret. Olive's retellings tended to be long. Besides what kind of interesting story could come from an ancient woman who had barely left Aunt Irene's in the past 15 years?

"You know how sometimes in the winter sheets of ice form on the edge of the river?"

"Yea."

"Well Grandmom told me that during one of her first winters living at Aunt Irene's, a dog got stuck out there. It was a black retriever. It loved to swim. Nobody knows why it went out there, but there he was half in the water hanging onto the edge of that ice."

Margaret remembered something about that. "Yes that was my Daddy's friend's dog. He did get out. He managed to pull himself out after they left him there. Nobody could bear to watch him die, so they walked home and they were barely home ten minutes when the dog came up to the back door. He was half frozen, half dead, and all exhausted. I've heard that story from the Prater's a dozen times."

"But he didn't pull himself out. He was rescued by a young girl only ten years old." Olive was happy to have a story to tell, and now she had their attention. "Grandmom watched the whole thing from Aunt Irene's family room window. The Praters and their neighbors seemed to be trying to figure out some way to reach out to the dog or get across the ice. Andrew tried to slide out on his belly but after a few feet he turned around and shimmied back to the beach. They even threw an inter tube tied to a rope but that didn't help. After about forty minutes of this they went away. Mrs. Prater was leaning on her husband, she was clearly upset. Not two minutes after they were out of sight a girl appeared on the river beach. She looked around as if making sure nobody could see what she was about to do. Then she got down and slowly slid out on that ice on her belly. She managed to get the dog onto the ice. Grandmom watched the dog run off and held her breath as the girl very slowly inched her way back to the beach."

The girls thought about that for a minute. Georgia was impressed by her sister's surprisingly good story.

"Wow, I'll bet she never took credit for the rescue because she knew she'd get in deep trouble for risking herself for a dog," Margaret said.

"Yes that's exactly what Grandmom and I thought," Olive added.

"Did Grandmom recognize the girl?," Georgia wanted to know.

"She did, it was Martha May." They were all quiet for a beat. Then Olive continued. "Now I figure that everybody has something wonderful about them, and everybody has something awful about them. Unfortunately many times only one or the other is recognized."

\* \* \*    \* \* \*

Georgia sat down for a break. Her friends and sister were still dancing. When would Jacob get here? She smoothed her hair again and scanned the crowd. Because her gaze was fixed far across the room, she didn't see Bobby until he briskly took the seat across from her. A pang struck. She hopped up not wanting to be seen sitting with him. He stood too not meaning to make her uncomfortable.

A rhythm and blues song was playing. The amazing voice of one of the Five Keys sang slowly:

*You've got to give a little, take a little*
*And let your poor heart break a little*
*That's the glory of, that's the story of love*

Bobby finally spoke; it was one of the rare times in his life when he didn't know what he was doing.

"It was, ah, good," he put his hand out to take hers but drew back quickly because it was clear that she wouldn't take his hand.

"Yes, it was good," Georgia responded quietly her eyes were filling up behind her small smile. The special time they had spent together was going to have to be enough.

And it would be enough. Neither Georgia nor Bobby would forget a moment of it. And so they always had each other. Those feelings would always be there, and they would always bring a peaceful smile.

"You take care of yourself, okay," she managed.

"Take care," he spoke softly. He had the same small smile. He too felt that what he shared with Georgia would never be over. They were bonded forever. For both Georgia and Bobby this feeling was a huge relief.

The amazing voice continued:

*As long as there's the two of us*
*We've got the world and all its charms*
*And when the world is through with us*
*We've got each others arms*

\* \* \*    \* \* \*

Jacob had spotted Georgia near the tables. A stranger was talking to his girl and she was obviously terrified. She's so sweet. "Hey, how's my girl? You look beautiful!" Before Jacob could think of anything clever to say to the stranger he had turned to leave. Only Georgia saw the happy tears in those tough-unbelievable-striking eyes.

It was maybe the single most incredible moment of her life thus far. Bobby was walking away, but she was happy! She knew she would always have him. Thank God Jacob was now embracing her. She needed something to hang on to. She might have fainted. Jacob, of course, handsome-responsible-talented-in love with her, Jacob. He made sense.

Jacob figured he was going to have to get used to other men being attracted to his woman. Especially that night. Holy smokes, he didn't remember ever seeing a woman look as beautiful as Georgia did right then. He relished for awhile in being so happy to see her. Georgia was starting to get embarrassed by the amount of affection she was getting in front of everybody.

"Would you like to go out on the deck?," Georgia asked sweetly.

"Yes, let's go."

Jacob was wearing a suit that she had never seen before. He also had a new haircut. They held hands and politely acknowledged thier friends as they made their way through the crowd. There were glass doors that opened to a large deck on the river beach. No one else was out there. Torches and candle light gave the deck only a little light. He led her to a cushioned bench only a few feet from the sand. A candle lamp hung nearby illuminating their faces.

"Georgia you really really, I mean look at you, your gorgeous," He stammered.

She smiled and said, "Thank you, I tried my best. You look great too." She leaned in for a kiss. He smelled good. And felt good. His hands were trying to be everywhere at once.

"Hey, just hold me for a minute, okay?," she whispered. And there it was again. Something seemed to be wrong with Georgia lately. He was not totally sure that she was happy with him. He was a little nervous about whether or not she would say yes. He actually decided to tell her about the house first then propose. Tonight looking at her in that devastating dress made him want to hear her to say yes more than anything in the world. He held her for a good long time.

Georgia enjoyed feeling safe and comfortable with Jacob. She knew she was where she belonged. The River breeze and the feel of that wide open space made their intimate time even more special. The enchanting voice of Ruth Brown floated to them gently from the dance hall. The stars and the brilliant moon looked down on this special scene.

They sat close now looking at each other in the candle light. There hands were together.

"So you really liked the house we've been working on, huh?," Jacob asked.

"Liked it? My goodness, Jacob, it's the most wonderful house I've ever been in! I love it! Absolutely love it!"

"That's good Honey, because it's my house. It's mine, I promise you." She gasped lightly, and it wasn't fake. Hearing him say those words struck her. His love for her was so sincere it almost came out of his pours. She knew he wanted her, *her*, so badly. It was painful and sweet to watch. She put her hand on his face. He kissed her hand and moved down to one knee.

"I'd like for it to be your house too." He pulled a ring out of his pocket and held it up. He was shaking. "Georgia Anne Sparks," just like he practiced, "you are the most amazing woman I will ever know. I am asking you for the great honor of being your husband. I promise …"

"Yes!," she leaped onto him. He toppled backwards and they were both on the wood of the deck.

"Yes?," he choked out.

"Yes!" His heart almost burst.

He needed to get that ring on her hand before he dropped it. They were both shaking now. They were silent for awhile, and then he scooped her up and stood. He swung his bride-to-be in an exuberant circle. Georgia could see now three girls pressed up against the glass door. Two of them were hopping up and down. She looked down at the ring that would be the focus of their evening. The stone was large and round. It was an excellently fine cut.

"I had Penn Jewelers make it for you. Do you like it?"

"Yes," Georgia was surprised by how her voice sounded. She decided to surrender to the happy tears. The girls could wait.

"Hey, you okay?"

"Yes," she squeaked, shaking still.

"Can you say anything besides 'yes'?"

She thought for a moment and then said, "yes." They both laughed. He hugged her close. He had never been this happy.

# Chapter Eleven

Bobby still came to Riverview Beach Park on business. Although Georgia continued to work there for another month they didn't see each other. He steered clear of her booth. He liked their goodbye and knew that some things are better left as they are.

Bobby continued his heavy involvement in his family's crimes. He became entrenched in the thick of it. He really had no choice. It was genuinely a blessing for him to die young. His was not a glamorous life. It was lonely, stressful, and completely dysfunctional. He lived in a tenth story two room apartment. It was always messy and Bobby was too proud to ever have visitors in. Most of his friends didn't even know exactly where he lived.

Shortly after saying goodbye to Georgia, Bobby developed a heroine habit. The drugs, however, didn't get a chance to kill him. He was wrongly accused of steeling from the family and was shot execution style. His murderer was a 19-year-old who was in fact Bobby's own first cousin. He didn't feel a thing. Bobby never had feelings for another woman after Georgia. Even with as short as their relationship was, you could say that she was the love of his life.

When he passed his Grandmother and Uncle were there to greet him. The pain and depression were gone. Bobby felt magnificent and loved. He had a knowledge and completeness that we will never understand while on this plain. One of the first things Bobby asked once on the other side was whether or not he would see Georgia again. He learned that eventually they would meet again, when Georgia came to the other side. Someone showed him how he could look in on Georgia and others he that he was interested in. When he saw Georgia she was holding a new baby. He knew the baby wasn't his, but the sight thrilled him just the same. He felt truly happy and blessed to see his beloved wife doing so well. Bobby now had full memory of their 35 year marriage and their Northern Missouri homestead. He found that everything felt wonderful on the other side. There was thorough love and enjoyment. Like most people he was not in a hurry to choose to start another life on 'our side'.

* * *    * * *

Only seven weeks after Jacob's proposal Jean Sparks helped her middle daughter into her white gown. The wedding was not more spectacular than Doris's. The green dresses and pink bouquets did look lovely but the only exceptional things were the bride and groom. Not only was Jacob a wonderful deserving man, he was lucky to have her. There are not many sweet, steady tempered beauties like Georgia. She would age beautifully.

Olive and Georgia remained close. Most weekends one of them would make the ten mile trip. Olive was thrilled with Georgia's wedding, the birth of her babies and the pomp surrounding each. Just as Georgia had felt about Doris' wedding and babies. Olive would marry and live in a charming old farm house on the Salem side of Lower Penns Neck. The town was renamed 'Pennsville' in the 1960's. Olive's pretty farm house overlooked the marshlands. She became enchanted by the beautiful swaying fragmities reeds, just as Georgia was enchanted by the River. Olive raised seven children on her Christmas tree farm, and would eventually become a beloved matriarchal figure in town. Olive would have twenty grandchildren who lived within five miles of her.

The large Victorian house on North Main Street in Woodstown became the center of family gatherings for both his side and hers. It was a magical setting for the treasured childhoods of their children. First came two boys, then a daughter.

She never spoke of it, but Georgia did come to terms with the incident on the River beach. It was something she looked back on with awe. She knew that she loved Bobby and had a special bond with him. The whole incident had made her become spiritual. The feelings she had for Bobby lasted long enough for her to suggest Robert as a handsome name for her second son. Someday when Georgia and Bobby meet again he will thank her for that. He'll tell her that although he followed the lives of all her children, he had special feelings for his namesake. He loves Robert as if he is his own son, and was the source of Robert's unnaturally good luck. Georgia still occasionally calls her daughter by the nickname, Peaches.

    \* \* \*  \* \* \*

  Even with as tremendous as her feelings for Bobby were, Georgia had so many many more that they practically buried him. She was graceful and adored by all. She lived in each moment and enjoyed her blessings every day. She led a charmed life. She was a deep ocean of happy times, love, and experiences. Her rich life was much deeper than the River that brought Bobby.

# More on Riverview Beach Park

## A Historic Study on Riverview Beach Park
## Pennsville, New Jersey

By Holly Bittle

### Those Ghosts

Wow! How can it be so quiet now and still!? For decades this emptiness buzzed with music, laughter, the chatter of thousands and the hustle of a huge daily routine. A routine that included the Wilson Line Steamships, the Pennsville-New Castle Ferry, a Park Train, spinning flashing amusements, the Dance Hall, a state of the art Olympic-sized pool, it all existed here. Just think of all the life, the friendships, the heart stopping, breath taking, laugh-till-you-hurt times that all those people had here. The gorgeous life guard she'd been dreaming of all Spring, scared toddlers on the carousel, the thrill of dropping down that enormous slide, these experiences times one million, they all happened here. The sound supposedly filled half of the town.

While standing in these quiet empty acres now it is unbelievable that those ghosts aren't strong enough. Shouldn't we be able to see something, or hear a sound? Maybe if we close our eyes and concentrate we can at least smell the food!

Holly Bittle<br>
Central Park Resident<br>
September, 2008

The American amusement park industry underwent a dramatic rise and fall in the beginning of the twentieth century. This was during a time when America was coming of age as an urban-industrial nation. New economic and social circumstances at work during this period were creating a more homogeneous American culture.[i] This rise of the amusement park industry was a product of the rise of the population in American cities. Seventy-five percent of the original American amusement parks that existed in 1920 did not survive until 1935.[ii] Any of these parks that survived the Great Depression are worth investigating. One such park, Riverview Beach Park, thrived throughout the period when most others were failing. Its clientele came mostly from Philadelphia by way of a magnificent fleet of ferry boats. Located in a rural part of southern New Jersey, the existence of this park had an effect on its surrounding community, Pennsville Township. Riverview Beach Park was one of the major contributing factors to the population growth and housing development of Pennsville Township during the mid-twentieth century.

The area known as Riverview Beach Park lies along the Delaware River close to the center of Pennsville Township, New

Jersey. Today, from the park there is a great view of the Delaware Memorial Bridge which lies about two miles to the North. Across the River is New Castle, Delaware. Pennsville is a quaint township of just under fourteen thousand residents. Pennsville still has many "Mom and Pop" owned businesses; there are three neighborhood elementary schools, a middle school, and our own Pennsville Memorial High School. Pennsville is the most populated township in Salem County but like the rest of the county the pace of life seems to be slower than that of neighboring Gloucester County. In fact, Salem County itself is an anomaly in New Jersey, being by far the least populated county. Salem County is so rural that it has half as many residents as the second least populated county in New Jersey.[iii] Pennsville is one of those places where it still feels like everybody knows each other. I have met many residents who have lived in Pennsville all their lives. Having lived in the town myself since my early twenties I have found that there really is no reason to leave town regularly. Many whole extended families live here. For these reasons Pennsville feels like its own little world.

This is a good central location between the cities of Wilmington, 12 miles to the west, Philadelphia 34 miles north west, and Atlantic City 63 miles south east. This area along the Deleware River now known as Pennsville has been colonized by Europeans for over 325 years. In the 1630's, Swedes and Finns living in Wilmington came across the Delaware to use this location for farming. Tribes of Lenni-Lenape lived here at that time. One of their leaders by the name of Obisquahassit sold large tracts of land to the settlers beginning in the 1660's. Principle occupations of Europeans in this area were fishing and farming.[iv]

Within the township there are six pre-Revolutionary homes built between 1726 and 1775 that are still being used as residences today. In 1837, the Federal government acquired land along the river in what is now the south side of town. A fort was built here to guard the mouth of the river. This fort, Fort Mott, is now part of a state park located in the township. During the seventeenth and eighteenth centuries the economy continued to be dominated by fishing and farming. There was shad fishing every spring, sturgeon fishing in the summer, in the fall they fished for catfish and eel then for carp in December. In the late seventeenth century, this section of the Delaware River was considered have the most plentiful sturgeon fishing in the world.[5] Some of the old fishing pier pilings can still be seen rising from the river.

This village on the river changed names several times and was known as Lower Penns Neck until residents voted to have it changed in 1965.[6] E.I. Dupont Chambers Works Plant opened in 1917 on the Northern end of Lower Penns Neck, known as Deepwater. This research and development company provided employment and stimulated growth to the area. Atlantic City Electric Company's Deepwater generating station was built in 1930. This provided power for the area as well as more employment. These remain two of the four major employers of Pennsville Township. The other two major employers are the Memorial Hospital of Salem County, and the township itself. The Delaware Memorial Bridge opened in August of 1951, and the twin span was opened in September of 1968. This opened up car traffic between Pennsville New Jersey and the area of Wilmington and New Castle Delaware.[7] This allowed Pennsville to become a bedroom community for the cities in Delaware.

Today in Pennsville the large 30 acre park lies mostly empty as cars file past it on Broadway (Route 49), the main thoroughfare. The area is open except for some large ancient trees and a few small ornamental ones people have planted along the trails. There is a good sized playground, a large picnic pavilion, a basketball court, a cinderblock bathroom building painted mural-style with scenes from the old amusement park, and a man made lake. These things look lost on the huge tract of land. These days the park is used mostly for walking, jogging, and family picnics. Twice a year carnivals are held on the grounds. One is the Township's huge Septemberfest celebration; the other is a smaller fair held in April with the typical carnival rides which benefits the Pennsville Midget Football League. There are a handful of other regular annual events held in the Riverview Beach Park including a Halloween costume contest, and a fishing contest. In its heyday this park drew as many as 42,000 people daily.

This area was used for entertainment as far back as the 1840's when a house that occupied the land there was used as a tavern, serving food and drink to travelers. In 1851 the tavern moved into a larger building called the Silver Grove Hotel. The hotel was so named because of the sixteen silver maple trees between it and the river. Next to the hotel was a picnic area, festivals were held there in the summer, and ice cream was served, and there was a large open pavilion.[8] In the days before air conditioning, being in a shady grove near open water was paradise on a hot day. The Silver Grove picnic area was only a small portion of the park as we know it today. Beginning in the 1850's, a boat called the Delaware made daily trips to this picnic ground from Philadelphia.[9]

In 1883 the Silver Grove Hotel and its picnic grounds were bought by Jacob and Margaret Acton. In 1889, the local farmers got together and held a large picnic on the grounds. This became an annual event called the Farmer's Picnic. The second year the farmers set up a human-powered merry-go-round. By the third year, a large horse powered merry-go-round was brought to the grounds. As the years passed, the picnic grounds acquired a few more novelties.[10] By the 1890's there were two excursion boats bringing people from Philadelphia daily.[11] In 1900, William (known as W.D.) Acton, Jacob and Margaret's grandson installed the first telephone at the hotel. From post-cards produced in the year 1909, we know that the grounds were then being called "Riverview" rather than "Silver Grove". The outdoor electric lights used in the park were the first in Lower Penns Neck. In 1912, an old ice house was turned into a merry-go-round house, the beautiful carousel it contained had three rows of horses. A young man named Harrison "Cuz" Hastings was put in charge of the merry-go-round house. He operated the carousel for the next 43 years.

In 1913, the Acton's bought a neighboring farm for $375.00 enlarging the Riverview property by several acres.[12] The amusement park began to take shape. At this time the festivities centered around the Merry-Go-Round building. In one corner of this building was a novelty stand, the other corners held a penny arcade, a refreshments stand, and a ski-ball alley. Nearby visitors could have their fortunes told and pictures taken in a building just north of the Merry-Go-Round building.[13]

In 1913, W. D. Acton inherited the property and his vision for the park increased multifold. The amusement park industry had become incredibly prosperous all across the country for the past few years. W. D. Acton's had ambitious dreams for his riverside park. He began making improvements right away. He had outbuildings moved to open up the park grounds, and had a row of bathhouses built along the beach. The wide and clean light sand beach was a beautiful spot for swimming. This was a great day trip location where city dwellers could spend their leisure time away from responsibilities. That summer an electric piano was put into the large pavilion.[14] I think that this might be the era when the park began to be known not just as Riverview, but as Riverview Beach. Before 1920, besides the beach there was also a dance hall, a few man powered amusements, a bowling alley, a novelty shop, and movies that were shown on certain nights of the week. The rides and movies cost park goers a five cents each.[15]

In 1922 W. D. Acton bought the 30 acre Baker farm which was just north of the existing park. He paid the widow, Mrs. Hannah Baker Batten $20,000.00, and agreed to allow her to live in her house on the property for the rest of her life. Shortly following this purchase the popularity of the park grew tremendously. In one day that same year, the boats with names such as the "City of Camden," "City of Philadelphia", "City of Wilmington", and "City of Chester" made their first trips to Mr. Acton's park.[16] This was the start of the constant ferry traffic that would continue for the next forty years. Cottages were already being built as summer or weekend homes for city families. These first cottages, or resort homes, were built to the south of the park along the river. Construction began on train track heading to the park.

1923 saw the start of the rapid addition of amusement attractions. The first new additions were the Hummingbird (the large roller coaster), Toyland,[17] the Eli Ferris Wheel, the Airplane Swings, a water slide, and a colossal dry slide.[18] The following year amusements named Old Mill, the Whip, Tilt-a-Whirl, scooters, and a small train were added.[19] W. D. Acton's park was becoming quite a phenomenon in this rural part of South Jersey. A large marshy area of the property was transformed into a 15 acre lake. The lake was used for fishing, boating, and ice skating in the winter. Visitors would rent paddle boats for a novel afternoon on the lake. On one occasion a pair of nuns visiting from Philadelphia fell out of their boat. Their habits were soaked but they were able to borrow bathing suits, and had a great time on the beach while their clothes were laundered by the locals.[20] This lake is one of the only two things from the amusement park that still exists there today.

By 1925 the old Merry-Go-Round building was made into a restaurant called the Casino.[21] Later this restaurant would be called the Mariner. The original carousel was replaced by a large Merry-Go-Round from the William Dentzel Company in Germantown Pennsylvania. This was only one of three carousels of its kind in the United States. It had four magnificent rows of animals. There were 63 horses, two serpent benches on the outer row along with one tiger and one lion. Because this carousel had "jumping" animals rather than stationary ones, it cost ten cents per ride, twice as much as a ride on the older carousel.[22] The older one was still in use; it had been moved from the center of the park and ran inside a barn. 1926 was the year that construction began on the Wilson Line's ferry slips on both the Riverview side and at New Castle Delaware.[23]

Seven new amusements were added in 1927 they were the battery operated Custer Cars, the Fun House, Glass House, Penny Arcade, Wildcat, Tumble Bug, and the Caterpillar. During the years of 1927 and 1928 the crowds at Riverview Beach swelled to 41,000 visitors per day. By this time the park had its own guard patrol.[24] The sandwiches served from the many scattered venders were supposed to be world class, and the smell of delicious food surrounded everything. About 300 people were employed at the park during the busy summer season. Many of the employees were teenagers. For a lot of people in this area, working in the park as a kid was a right of passage. During the off season, the remaining employees maintained the ground and the amusements.[25] A kiddie swimming pool was built in 1930. In 1934, a liquor license was obtained by the Silver Grove Hotel. Old and young alike loved to travel to this park from their city homes. The following is an excerpt from an article that ran in the Sampler on June 9, 1993. A woman named Eleanor C. Zane recounted her fond childhood memories of riding the Wilson Line Boats to the park.

> *-I remember well the wonderful sleek lines of the state of Delaware as it pulled into dock. Waiting at Fourth Street Wharf, anticipating the adventure before us, I could feel the excitement. -This was the home port of some of the finest steamships on the Delaware. –One of my favorite rides was the roller coaster (the little one, called the Wild Cat, 'cause the big one, the Hummingbird, was just too scary for a nine year old). I also liked the Whip, the Custer Cars, the train, the Ferris Wheel, and the Donkeys. Of course, I loved them all, but no visit to the park would be complete without a ride on the wonderful carousel. As I grew older, I spent some time in the olympic sized pool, and the skating rink, and I learned to love the Penny Arcade. Oh, what great memories I have of those days.*[26]

The next year, 1935, a man named Lawrence Chrisman from Schenectady, New York came to Riverview Beach to be the new park manager. He had previously been in charge of an amusement park in Bridgeport Connecticut, and had built roller coasters in different locations across the United States. Chrisman replaced Albert Hammond and eventually would become part owner of the park. The new manager first set out designing an Olympic-sized pool which would occupy the area of the duck pond. The 75' x 150' pool was completed in 1937.[27] This was a very popular attraction. It was advertised as one of the best pools in the country. The building that surrounded the pool was constructed beautifully. The depth of the water ranged from twelve feet to three feet. A state of the art filtration system circulated the water so that it was completely changed three times per day.[28] Acton's park remained prosperous through the Great Depression. By the 1930's the American amusement park industry had collapsed. Only about fifteen percent of parks the original parks remained in use.[29] In 1941, more new additions were erected in the park. These included the Flying Scooters, the Bubble Bounce, and a Hammond electric organ which played in the roller skating rink. This rink was formerly a dance hall. In 1943, the area is officially named Riverview Beach Park. Previously it was simply Riverview Beach. In 1948 new kiddie rides are added; they were the Miniature Whip, Fire Engines, and Miniature Flying Scooters.[30]

When the Delaware Memorial Bridge opened to traffic in 1951, visitors from the cities did not have to rely on ferry ships to make the trip to the park. Up until 1953 the park was owned by partners William D. Acton and Lawrence Chrisman. Both partners sold their shares that year. W. D. Acton sold to Alvis Wallace and Chrisman sold to Frank Morton. In 1955, the fleet of Wilson Line ferry ships were sold along with their wharves to the City Investing Company of New York City. Only two years later this company sold two of the ships for a sum of $700,000 to a company called Riverview Lines.[31] Some older Pennsville residents would say that 1958 marked the beginning of the end for the old park. This was the year that the new administration decided to fence the whole park and charge an admission fee. Township residents did not like this because they enjoyed having the freedom to walk into the park anytime. Things would never be the same after 1960 when the Wilson Line steamships crossed the Delaware for the last time.[32] Still, during the 1960's many visitors were enjoying Riverview Beach Park. The following are the words of Susan Bittle who fondly remembers visiting the park as a child during the 1960's.

> *I lived my first 19 years in Carney's Point Township (a neighbor of Pennsville). Growing up, Riverview Beach Park was a big part of my life. In the early 1960's one of my favorite memories was of seeing Sally Star at the park. What a treat!! I remember wearing my own cowgirl outfit, complete with holster, guns, and a cowgirl hat. My cousins were from Pennsville, when I would visit them we would go to the park pool. It was the biggest pool I had ever seen! We would get our hand stamped with a purple dye. The dye was only seen when we put our hand under special lights. This is how they could tell that we had paid for our visit to the pool. My cousins spent so much time in that pool that their hair turned green! Also, my great-grandparents celebrated their 50th wedding anniversary in the park in August of 1947. I have pictures of the building at the picnic grove, and a newspaper clipping about this event. My husband was from Swedesboro (about 10 miles from Pennsville) each year for their birthdays, he and his sister were taken to Riverview Beach Park to enjoy all the rides. Now my son and daughter-in-law live in Pennsville, and when we ride by the park I can still see the wooden rollercoaster!* [33]

By the sixties, the amusements were all old and many were badly in need of repair. The park closed and was torn down in 1967. William Foster was one of the men who was contracted to tear down the amusements. The following is excerpts from his first hand account as recorded in the book, Fond Memories.

> *-Most of the things like the cars and donkeys and mirrors were sold to whoever came along and wanted them. –It tore my heart up to have to tear those things down. I remember the archway at the entrance had been sold to a man, but he died before he could take it, so I just left it there - When I tore down the rest rooms I found a lot of change underneath, you wouldn't believe how much I found. When I think about the Park I think the end came when they put up that fence. The local people didn't like that. The company that owned it last didn't want to spend money for parts or for anything. What a shame.*[34]

The archway that William Foster left standing is the second thing that still remains from the old days. Or maybe it is not. For many the memories they have from Riverview Beach Park will always remain. These were the times of their lives. Parks devoted to having a great time are very important.

Humans are not meant to spend their lives only toiling away at work. Life shouldn't always be serious. Some people in the early twentieth century appreciated the significance of amusement parks. John Nolen published in 1910 that these parks were of "inestimable worth. He went on to call them a "necessity to the health of urban populations, they are indispensable and should be selected and developed by experts."[35] Public amusements are a show of respect for the part of us that needs to have fun. They are huge monuments to the human need to enjoy life.

Although outdoor amusements have not always included complex mechanical rides, they have been part of European culture for the past four hundred years. Some of the earliest public amusement parks were London's pleasure gardens. In the late seventeenth and early eighteenth centuries these novel parks were highly illuminated at night. Visitors enjoyed elaborate landscaping, refreshment stands, balloon rides, concerts, theater performances, sports, social dancing and fireworks. At these pleasure gardens all classes mingled together. [36] During the nineteenth century the United States as well as some European countries held World's Fairs or World's Expositions. Originally these fairs were educational in nature. They would exhibit the latest technology, the things that the host city was most proud of. These events were highly anticipated.

In an article titled "The World's Fair of 1892" Edward Atkinson, the director of a previous exposition is quoted on his predictions on the upcoming event. There is no mention in this article about amusement rides. It seems that up until that year most of the expositions had been a display of goods and science exhibits only, and did not include amusements at all. The theme for the World's Fair of 1892 would be the four hundredth year anniversary of the European discovery of the New World. Because of this theme, Atkinson predicted that the exhibition would show the progression of art and industry from 1492 until the present day.[37] This fair, held in Chicago, proved to be very influential to the amusement park industry.

The organizers of this fair were aware that uninvited amusements often appeared near an official exposition. For example, during the 1876 centennial fair held in Philadelphia, a whole array of amusements were set up across the street. They offered beer, peanuts, and side show attractions including intelligent pigs, a five-legged cow, and a 602 pound fat lady.

Recognizing the importance of amusements, and probably aware of their potential for profit, the directors decided to arrange their own amusement district separate from the educational exhibits.[38] This was an amazing display that would set the standard for all fairs to follow. The amusement section was called the midway. This was a mile long strip of concessions and entertainment. Its theme was an exotic mix of cultures from around the world. There was a mosque, camel rides, Blarney Castle, and an African village among many others. The human exotic or freak show elements were made more acceptable by being called "anthropological exhibits."[39] Its most striking feature had to have been the original ferris wheel. Created by George Washington Gale Ferris it was an engineering feat by any standards. At 264 feet tall, the wheel carried 36 huge cars, each car could hold 60 passengers. Therefore each 20 minute ride could be enjoyed by as many as 2,160 people![40] The construction cost was $350,000 but it could be recovered within a few weeks. Fairgoers paid a hefty fee of 50 cents per ride, which was equal to the admission price of the fair. Following the huge sensation of the 1892 World's Fair, rides, games, strange exhibits, and the ferris wheel would be staples at any fair or amusement park.[41]

Meanwhile other forces were shaping the American amusement parks. Beginning in the 1890's trolley companies started to build amusement attractions at the end of their lines. The lure of the parks promoted ticket sales during weekends. These would be the original American amusement parks. Since the trolley companies only paid a flat fee for the electricity they used, it did not cost them extra money to run mechanical rides and lights.[42] These trolley parks were often located in shady picnic groves near a body of water. These were cool places to visit on hot weekends, blending natural and man made pleasures. People living in American cities were ready for this new type of pass time. These parks were so successful that they caused the price of daily transit to go down. They rapidly expanded and in the first few years of the twentieth century they included dance halls, sports fields, boat rides, and restaurants, along with the ever present mechanical rides. An article that ran in Cosmopolitan magazine in 1902 stated that the trolley parks sometimes had 50,000 visitors per day.[43] The trolley parks sprung up so quickly that still early in the twentieth century every major American city had at least one of these parks. By 1920 there were 2,000 of these parks in the United States. Near New York City was Palisades Park, New Jersey, near Philadelphia was Willow Grove Park, and San Francisco had a trolley park called The Chutes.[44] Originally they all included a dance pavilion of some kind. As years passed they grew to incorporate elements taken from the wildly prosperous Coney Island.

      Coney Island contained three separate parks which competed fiercely with each other, causing innovation.[45] These parks dominated the American amusement park industry in "size, scope, and fame".[46] The first of Coney Island's influential parks was Steeple Chase, which included rides and circuslike entertainment. The second was Luna Park, which offered visitors spectacular shows featuring horror, disaster, and live experiences. These live experience shows included the repeated burning of a five story building complete with flames, people jumping out of the windows into nets; another one time show featured the electrocution death of an ageing elephant. Dreamland was the last park to be built on Coney Island. It appealed to a more educated crowd, with its stunning architecture. This park upheld the bourgeois norms of decency. At night the lights from Dreamland could be seen from miles away. During the latter years of the nineteenth century Coney Island was not family friendly. There were brothels and saloons where there was plenty of gambling and boxing. However, through a change of management and a conscious effort to reform the island it became a different environment by the early twentieth century.[47] Coney Island's parks were at the forefront of amusement technology and had a huge effect on the industry. Amusement rides were becoming a symbol of American life. Beginning in the 1920's immigrants coming to America for the first time saw Coney Island's huge ferris wheel before they saw the statue of Liberty.[48]

City dwellers all over the nation were enjoying carousels, ferris wheels, roller coasters, and penny arcades during the day. In the evenings they enjoyed dining, fireworks, dancing and music. During these early years most parks did not permit alcohol on their grounds and people dressed in their Sunday best. Men wore suits, ties, and hats.[49] Very carful consideration was taken to insure that the music played at these parks was fitting of the event. If the main attraction was dancing, the crowd would expect a brass band. In many places refreshments would be served at a respectful distance from where the musicians were playing so that people who wanted to listen would not be distracted.[50] Dancing and music were essential factors in people's attraction to amusement parks.

In the early twentieth century people of every social class in every city loved dancing. It was not uncommon for single women to go out dancing two or three nights per week.[51] The ads luring visitors to an amusement park were very specific about what music would be playing. A small ad that ran in the *Salem Standard and Jerseyman* in May of 1925 invites people to come to Riverview Beach, New Jersey to enjoy "Dancing in the Evening music by Hendrickson's Louisville Serenaders Nine Piece Orchestra." The "Amusements of the Latest Type" are mentioned at the bottom of the ad, showing how powerful the lure of the music was compared to that of the rides. [52,53] Leisure time spent on dancing and other recreation was evidence of the major changes happening across the country.

 The rise of American amusements was tied very closely to the huge expansion of American cities between 1870 and 1920. During that fifty year span, the urban population of the U.S. grew from less that ten million to over fifty four million residences. More Americans were able to enjoy this type of recreation in the early twentieth century because the workforce had gone through dramatic changes. American's holding "white collar" positions increased most dramatically. Far fewer Americans worked on farms causing the cities to expand rapidly. The cost of living decreased by 50% between the years of 1870 and 1920. This caused a steady decrease in the number of hours people had to work per week. The American clerical workforce grew from 160,000 in 1880 to over 1.7 million in 1910. Since a large number of Americans were doing clerical work they could afford go out at night and still get to work on time. This was opposed to farm and factory workers who had to wake up at 5:00 am.[54] Working in an office did not leave a person as physically exhausted as working on a farm or other manual labor. Clerical work left a person with more of a desire to go out on evenings and weekends. Due to the development of unions and advancements in industrialization people who were still doing factory work were working less hours per week.[55] In addition, more average people were able to afford to go on a daytrip because people living in cities had more expendable income. America was changing from the ninetieth century economy based on labor and production, to the twentieth century economy based on the consumption of products and leisure activities.[56] Recreation began to be thought of as a necessity. According to the United States Census Bureau, wages increased significantly from 1890 to 1925, possibly due to the economic stimulus from World War I. After 1920 the price of food declined, providing even more expendable income.[57] The rapid growth of American amusement parks came from a demand for this type of recreation. The demand came from a large urban public who was able to pay for amusement and who wanted to see the newest attractions. This industry was the most prominent feature of the changing nature of American culture. The authority of genteel Victorian values was crumbling. Americans belonging to all classes were apt to enjoy the exuberant, sensual, and uninhibited environment offered by these parks.[58]

The height of activity in American amusement parks followed World War I. It was as if a single celebration was being enjoyed across the country. In 2,000 places in or near the cities, Americans were having a great time on very similar rides in very similar parks. However, as so often is the story, what goes up must come down. During the twenties, the industry began a steady decline. Factors in this decline included the extensive railroad strike in 1921, and the popularity of the automobile. It became the trend for families to take vacations to visit different locations. It was no longer enviable to visit the park at the end of the railroad track where everyone had been. Most of the city amusement parks did not have parking lots to accommodate visitors traveling by car. Also during the twenties there was three consecutive years of bad summer weather. Because of the bad weather people changed their habits and found other ways to spend their summer weekends. Then the Great Depression began at the end of the decade. Average Americans no longer had expendable income to spend money in the parks.[59]

Within fifteen years the number of American amusement parks changed dramatically. The 2,000 parks that existed in 1920 dwindled to only 303 in 1935. City life began to change again. It became a trend for the people who did have money to leave the cities for suburban life. American cities became home to minorities. In the 1940's and 1950's the affluent visitors still coming to amusement parks were put off by the number of minorities who were visiting the parks. This affluent population did not care to mingle with, or be equated with, the inner city population. By the 1950's most households had a television providing a new form of entertainment. The forces working against public amusements were powerful and all encompassing.[60] The decline of the American amusement park industry was so complete that any park that survived this era is worth investigating. Only a small handful remained in the 1950's. Riverview Beach Park survived into the 1960's. However, what makes it even more unique is that it was gaining popularity during the years when the great majority of all American amusement parks were failing.

The existence of Riverview Beach Park influenced the population growth of the surrounding township. During the seventy years leading up to the 1920's the population growth had fluctuated between -9.4% to 11.3%, with an average of 1.6% growth per decade. Around 1920 the population of Lower Penns Neck spiked tremendously to a population increase of 39.2% in ten years. Between the years of 1920 to 1930 the population grew by 36.5%. Between the years of 1930 to 1940 the growth was 74.3%, and for the next two decades the population growth averaged 42.8% per decade. Between the years of 1960 and 1970 the population growth was 27.6%, corresponding to the decline of the amusement park. After 1970, the amusement park no longer existed. The percentage of population growth between the years of 1970 to 1980 was only 4.2%.[61] This evidence definitely shows a large positive fluctuation in population growth during the years that correspond to the height of activity at the Riverview Beach Park. However, we need to look at what else was happening in this area between the years of 1910 and 1970.

It is necessary to look at the population growth for the two river front townships to the North of Pennsville to see how they compared. The neighboring township to the North of Pennsville is Carney's Point. According to the United States Census Bureau, this township actually had a significant negative population decrease from 1920 to 1930, -38%. This is a great contrast to Lower Penns Neck which grew in population during that period by 36.5%. Between the years of 1930 to 1940, both townships showed high population increases but that of Lower Penns Neck was 50.4% higher than that of Carney's Point. During the decade in question the population growth for Salem County as a whole was very low. The United States Census Bureau shows 36,834 total Salem County residents in 1930 and 42,274 Salem County residents in 1940. The total increase in population for Salem County was 5,440 individuals in ten years, an increase of less than 8%. During those same ten years Lower Penns Neck's population increased by 36.5%.[62]

It seems as though residents were moving into Pennsville from within the county. At first glance it may seem like this growth could be attributed to the two large employers Atlantic City Electric and E. I. Dupont. However, Atlantic City Electric began its operation in 1917 a few years prior to the huge influx of people and E. I. Dupont did not open until 1930 so it cannot be used to explain the dramatic increase during the 1920's. The Delaware Memorial Bridge cannot be used to explain the population increase during the 1920's because its construction had not yet begun. It may be that people were moving off of the farms within the center of the county, and moving to the towns in what is known as "the corridor" along the River. If this is true, the farmers were choosing to move to Lower Penns Neck over the other townships. Although this is not a totally conclusive study on all the factors that may have contributed to the large population fluctuation in this area, the amusement park was one of the contributing factors.

This is quite clear because many homes built in Pennsville during the mid twentieth century were not primary residences. The park influenced the development of houses in Lower Penns Neck in two ways. First, houses were built as weekend or summer homes for city residents, and the housing developments advertised their building lots as being part of a resort community because of Riverview Beach Park. Many people who lived in Wilmington and Philadelphia built weekend or vacation homes near Riverview Beach Park. These homes were built on either side of the park on the river side of Broadway. Usually referred to as cottages, they were small and lacked insulation for cold weather. On the narrow river front lots, the cottages were usually two stories. The cottages built on the streets not considered to be river front typically were small ranch style houses. This began as early as early as 1914, and continued into the 1950's.[63] Most of these cottages are still being used as residences today; all at some point were updated with insulation.

The farm immediately to the North of the park began to be developed in 1925. This thirty acre farm was known as the Brandriff track, but today is known as central park neighborhood. An ad for these home sites which ran in two Philadelphia newspapers in 1925.

> *Ideal Home Sites! The Wise Investor Buys at the Brandriff Tract! Excellent for homes or cottages near fastest growing summer resort! The new FERRY means that real estate values will steadily climb!"* [64]

A map of this area dated 1960 shows the growth of the neighborhoods near the park. By this date, the Brandriff track included five avenues approximately a quarter of a mile long running perpendicular between Broad Street and the river, and one avenue running parallel to Broad Street through the neighborhood. There were approximately 150 new homes in the Brandriff track by 1960. Just north of that development, two more avenues running perpendicular to Broad Street had been formed, Marlyn and Jenkins. These two streets include at least twenty homes that were built as secondary homes mixed with others whose original purpose was a primary residence. This area was previously a farm belonging to Joel H. Jenkins, Senior. South of this, between Broadway and the River is a development of larger brick ranch homes these were mostly built as primary residences. Meanwhile, on the other side of Broadway two farms owned by Edward Pinson and Sedgewick Dolbow had been sold for housing development. These streets on the North side of the park are now known as Central Park neighborhood. From the map we can see that the homes are about evenly distributed on either side of Broadway by 1960. From the map we can estimate there are over 400 homes existing in central park in 1960 that did not exist in 1920.[65][66]

On the Southern side of the park is the oldest section of Pennsville the area around Main Street, and Ferry Road. Just South of that is a small housing development called Castleview Hights that was created in 1916. This was advertised by the Trinity Land and Improvement Company as seven hundred and seventy building lots. The street names are Castle Hights Avenue, High Land Ave, and Dunn Lane. Although the land was dry, at a good elevation, and the sales promotion included a hot air balloon ascension that drew a crowd, this development was a flop. Very few homes were built. Apparently in 1916 there was not as big of a draw to this area as there would be after 1925. [67][68] In the decades to follow the amusement park drew people to the area.

South of Castleview Hights is a very large neighborhood between Broadway and the River. This area is about three times larger than what exists between Broadway and the River on the North side because just south of the park Broadway takes a sharp curve toward the east away from the River. This low lying area is known as Penn Beach. The advertising campaign for home sights in this area began in 1926. These ads ran in the Philadelphia record. Penn Beach is by far the largest neighborhood in town. By 1960, Penn Beach included twenty-two streets running perpendicular to the river beach and forty three streets running parallel to the river beach. The perpendicular streets are roughly a mile long and many of the parallel streets are over a half mile long. With an average lot width of 100 feet, this equates to well over one thousand Penn Beach homes. By 1960, there was another small housing development on the West side of Broad Street across from Penn Beach. This development called Valley Park, was comprised mostly of homes with three and four split levels and included seven streets by 1960.[69]

Present day Pennsville took shape during those years. The neighborhood elementary schools of Pennsville are Penn Beach, Valley Park, and Central Park Elementary Schools. The housing developments in Lower Penns Neck were hugely successful during the years that the amusement park was in its prime. The housing development campaign called Castleview Hights that was attempted prior to the era of the large scale amusement rides was clearly not as successful. There has not been any large scale housing development in Pennsville since the time of the Amusement park.[70]

The Riverview Beach Amusement Park brought something special to Pennsville Township. It was that spirit of fun, the importance of not taking life too seriously, this was the important lesson that amusement parks offered to America. These parks were fundamental in the development of American popular culture. They provided a place to experiment with the boundaries between pleasure and decency, and a place where a day could be devoted to enjoyment.[71] This spirit of fun thrived in America during the beginning of the twentieth century, making some people millionaires, and making millions of people happy. And of course, what could be more important than enjoying life. In some ways this spirit is still alive in Pennsville today. The park which stands empty like a giant memorial is home to large amusement rides twice a year. Every September and April the music, chatter, laughter, rides, the food, and most importantly, the fun is there again. It rings out through the breeze from the River on those days and once again the sound fills half of the town.

End Notes

[i] John F. Kasson, *Amusing the Million* (New York: Hill and Wang, 1978), 3-4.

[ii] Judith A. Adams, *The American Amusement Park Industry: A History of Technology and Thrills* (Twayne Publications, 1991), 66.

[3] The U. S. Census Bureau, Sections; "New Jersey: The Population of Counties by Decennial Census: 1900 to 1990," http:www.census.gov.

[4] Mary F. Sanderlin, *Stories of Lower Penns Neck: A Background of Pennsville Township* (Pennsville: Pennsville Township Historical Society, 1994) 2-6.

[5] Mary F. Sanderlin, *Stories of Lower Penns Neck: A Background of Pennsville Township*, 32.

[6] Mary F. Sanderlin, *Stories of Lower Penns Neck: A Background of Pennsville Township*, 23-26.

[7] Pennsville Township Historical Society, *Fond Memories: Thoughts and photos from the employees of Riverview Beach Park* (Pennsville: Pennsville Township Historical Society, 1998) 9.

[8] Mary F. Sanderlin, *Stories of Lower Penns Neck: A Background of Pennsville Township*, 141.

[9] Pennsville Township Historical Society, *Fond Memories: Thoughts and photos from the employees of Riverview Beach Park*, 9.

[10] Mary F. Sanderlin, *Stories of Lower Penns Neck: A Background of Pennsville Township*, 141.

[11] Pennsville Township Historical Society, *Fond Memories: Thoughts and photos from the employees of Riverview Beach Park*, 29.

[12] Mary F. Sanderlin, *Stories of Lower Penns Neck: A Background of Pennsville Township*, 9.

[13] Mary F. Sanderlin, "Riverview Park Opened 50 Years Ago this Week –A Meca for Funsters," *The Pennsville Progress*, (1960's?).

[14] Pennsville Township Historical Society, *A Pictorial Review of the Township of Pennsville Past and Present* (Pennsville: Pennsville Township Historical Society, 1988) 29.

[15] Mary F. Sanderlin, *Stories of Lower Penns Neck: A Background of Pennsville Township*, 135.

[16] Pennsville Township Historical Society, *Fond Memories: Thoughts and photos from the employees of Riverview Beach Park*, 9.

[17] Pennsville Township Historical Society, *Fond Memories: Thoughts and photos from the employees of Riverview Beach Park*, 7.

[18] Mary F. Sanderlin, *Stories of Lower Penns Neck: A Background of Pennsville Township*, 138.

[19] Pennsville Township Historical Society, *Fond Memories: Thoughts and photos from the employees of Riverview Beach Park*, 7.

[20] Pennsville Township Historical Society, *Fond Memories: Thoughts and photos from the employees of Riverview Beach Park*, 90.

[21] Mary F. Sanderlin, *Stories of Lower Penns Neck: A Background of Pennsville Township*, 138.

[22] Pennsville Township Historical Society, *A Pictorial Review of the Township of Pennsville Past and Present*, 56.

[23] Pennsville Township Historical Society, *Fond Memories: Thoughts and photos from the employees of Riverview Beach Park*, 8.

[24] Pennsville Township Historical Society, *Fond Memories: Thoughts and photos from the employees of Riverview Beach Park*, 8.

[25] Mary F. Sanderlin, *Stories of Lower Penns Neck: A Background of Pennsville Township*, 138.

[26] Eleanor C. Zane, "Wilson Line, Riverview Beach Park Memories," *The Sampler*, June 9, 1993.

[27] Pennsville Township Historical Society, *A Pictorial Review of the Township of Pennsville Past and Present*, 8, 76.

[28] Mary F. Sanderlin, *Stories of Lower Penns Neck: A Background of Pennsville Township,* 138.

[29] Raymond M. Weinstein, "Disneyland and Coney Island: Reflections on the Evolution of the Modern Amusement Park," *Journal of Popular Culture,* Vol. 26, 1, (summer 1992):145.

[30] Pennsville Township Historical Society, *Fond Memories: Thoughts and photos from the employees of Riverview Beach Park,* 10.

[31] Pennsville Township Historical Society, *Fond Memories: Thoughts and photos from the employees of Riverview Beach Park,* 12.

[32] Pennsville Township Historical Society, *Fond Memories: Thoughts and photos from the employees of Riverview Beach Park,* 18.

[33] Susan Bittle, Interviewed by author, October 15, 2008.

[34] Pennsville Township Historical Society, *Fond Memories: Thoughts and photos from the employees of Riverview Beach Park,* 99.

[35] John Nolen, "The Parks and Recreation Facilities in the United States," *Annals of the American Academy of Political and Social Science,* Vol. 35, 2 ( March 1910): 1.

[36] Raymond M. Weinstein, 131-164.

[37] American Association for the Advancement of Science, "The World's Fair of 1892," *Science,* Vol. 14, No. 343, Aug. 1889, 146.

[38] David Nasaw, *Going Out: The Rise and Fall of Public Amusements* (Harvard University Press, 1999) 67.

[39] Judith A. Adams, 29.

[40] Judith A. Adams, 19.

[41] Raymond M. Weinstein, 133.

[42] Raymond M. Weinstein, 132.

[43] Judith A. Adams, 57.

[44] Warner Home Video/ PBS Home Video, *Great Old Amusement Parks, 1999.*

[45] Raymond M. Weinstein, 131-133.

[46] John F. Kasson, 7.

[47] Raymond M. Weinstein, 152-155.

[48] Warner Home Video/ PBS Home Video, *Great Old Amusement Parks*, 1999.

[49] Judith A. Adams, 59.

[50] Philip H. Geopp, "Music and Refreshments in Parks," *Annals of the American Academy of Political and Social Science*, Vol. 35, No. 2, (March 1910): 170-176.

[51] Judith A. Adams, 105.

[52] "Come to Riverview Beach," *Salem Standard and Jerseyman*, May 27, 1925, Pennsville Township Historical Society, Riverview Beach Park folder.

[53] "Grand Opening Riverview Beach," *Salem Standard and Jerseyman*, May 20, 1925, Pennsville Township Historical Society, Riverview Beach Park folder.

[54] David Nasaw, 3-5.

[55] Judith A. Adams, 60-66.

[56] Raymond M. Weinstein, 160.

[57] Judith A. Adams, 61.

[58] John F. Kasson, 6-7

[59] Judith A. Adams, 66.

[60] Judith A. Adams, 66.

[61] The U. S. Census Bureau, Sections; "New Jersey: The Population of Pennsville Township by Decennial Census: 1900 to 1990," http:www.census.gov.

[62] The U. S. Census Bureau, Sections; "New Jersey: The Population of Counties by Decennial Census: 1900 to 1990," "New Jersey: The Population of Pennsville Township by Decennial Census: 1900 to 1990," "New Jersey: the Population of Carney's Point Township by Decennial Census: 1900 to 1990," "New Jersey: the Population of Penns Grove by Decennial Census: 1900 to 1990," and "New Jersey: Resident Population and Apportionment of the U. S. House of Representatives", http:www.census.gov.

[63] Mary F. Sanderlin, *Stories of Lower Penns Neck: A Background of Pennsville Township*, 136-7.

[64] "Advertising Campaign for the Brandriff Tract," newspaper unknown, 1925, Pennsville Historical Society, Neighborhoods folder.

[65] John L. Reeves, "Revised Zoning Map of Lower Penns Neck Township", April 1960.

[66] Mary F. Sanderlin, *Stories of Lower Penns Neck: A Background of Pennsville Township*, 136-7.

[67] John L. Reeves, "Revised Zoning Map of Lower Penns Neck Township", April 1960.

[68] Mary F. Sanderlin, *Stories of Lower Penns Neck: A Background of Pennsville Township,* 136-7.

[69] John L. Reeves, "Revised Zoning Map of Lower Penns Neck Township", April 1960.

[70] Mary F. Sanderlin,, *Stories of Lower Penns Neck: A Background of Pennsville Township,* 136-7.

[71] Jon Sterngass, First Resorts: *Pursuing Pleasure at Saratoga Springs, Newport, & Coney Island* (Baltimore: John Hopkins University Press, 2001) 8.

## Bibliography

Primary Sources

Ads

1. "Come to Riverview Beach," *Salem Standard and Jerseyman,* May 27, 1925, Pennsville Township Historical Society, Riverview Beach Park folder.

2. "Grand Opening Riverview Beach," *Salem Standard and Jerseyman,* May 20, 1925, Pennsville Township Historical Society, Riverview Beach Park folder.

3. "Advertising Campaign for the Brandriff Tract," newspaper unknown, 1925, Pennsville Historical Society, Neighborhoods folder.

Articles

4. American Association for the Advancement of Science, "The World's Fair of 1892," *Science*, Vol. 14, No. 343, Aug. 1889, 146-147.

5. Geopp, Philip H., "Music and Refreshments in Parks," *Annals of the American Academy of Political and Social Science*, Vol. 35, No. 2 (March 1910):170-176.

6. Nolen, John, "The Parks and Recreation Facilities in the United States," *Annals of the American Academy of Political and Social Science*, Vol. 35, No. 2, March 1910, 1-12.

7. Platt, William J., "A Note on Amusement Park Economics," *Journal of the Operations Research Society of America*, Vol. 3, No. 1, (Feb. 1955):101-103.

8. Zane, Eleanor C., "Wilson Line, Riverview Beach Park Memories," *The Sampler*, June 9, 1993.

Book

9. Pennsville Township Historical Society, *Fond Memories: Thoughts and photos from the employees of Riverview Beach Park* (Pennsville: Pennsville Township Historical Society, 1998).

Maps

10. Pennsville Township Historical Society, Map folder, "Map of Lower Penns Neck Township 1865."

11. Reeves, John L., "Revised Zoning Map of Lower Penns Neck Township", April 1960.

Postcard

12. Salem County Historical Society, Riverview Beach Park Folder, "New $150,000 Pool Riverview Beach, Pennsville, N.J." date and author unknown.

Interview

13. Susan Clements Bittle, interviewed by Holly Bittle on her memories of Riverview Beach Park, October 15, 2008.

Website

14. The U. S. Census Bureau, Sections; "New Jersey: The Population of Counties by Decennial Census: 1900 to 1990," "New Jersey: The Population of Pennsville Township by Decennial Census: 1900 to 1990," "New Jersey: the Population of

Carney's Point Township by Decennial Census: 1900 to 1990," "New Jersey: the Population of Penns Grove by Decennial Census: 1900 to 1990," and "New Jersey: Resident Population and Apportionment of the U. S. House of Representatives", http:www.census.gov.

Secondary Sources

Articles

1. Nye, Russel B., "Eight Ways of Looking at an Amusement Park," *The Journal of Popular Culture*, Vol. 15, 1 (winter 1981):63-75.

2. Sanderlin, Mary F., "Riverview Park Opened 50 Years Ago this Week –A Mecca for Funsters," *The Pennsville Progress*, (1960's?).

3. Weinstein, Raymond M., "Disneyland and Coney Island: Reflections on the Evolution of the Modern Amusement Park," *Journal of Popular Culture*, Vol. 26, 1 (summer 1992):131-164.

4. Rabinovitz, Lauren, "Urban Wonderlands: Sitting Modernity in turn-of-the-century Amusement Parks," *European Contributions to American Studies*, Vol. 45, (2001):85-97.

5. Snow, Robert E. and Wright, David E., "Coney Island: A Case Study in Popular Culture and Technological Change," *Journal of Popular Culture,* Vol. 9, 4, (summer 1976):960-975.

Books

6. Adams, Judith A., *The American Amusement Park Industry: A History of Technology and Thrills* (Twayne Publications, 1991).

7. Kasson, John F., *Amusing the Million* (Hill and Wang, New York, 1978).

8. Nasaw, David, *Going Out: The Rise and Fall of Public Amusements* (Harvard University Press, 1999).

9. Pennsville Township Historical Society, *A Pictorial Review of the Township of Pennsville Past and Present* (Pennsville: Pennsville Township Historical Society, 1988).

10. Sanderlin, Mary F., *Stories of Lower Penns Neck: A Background of Pennsville Township* (Pennsville: Pennsville Township Historical Society, 1994).

11. Sterngass, Jon, First Resorts: *Pursuing Pleasure at Saratoga Springs, Newport, & Coney Island* (Baltimore: John Hopkins University Press, 2001).

Video

12. Warner Home Video/ PBS Home Video, *Great Old Amusement Parks*, 1999.

## About the Author

Holly Bittle lives in Woodstown, NJ with her husband and two children. She has a B.A. in History from Rowan University. Holly works part time at the local elementary school and is a member of the Junior Woman's Club of Woodstown. She enjoys reading and writing. *The River Beach* is her first novel.

## More to Come

Look for *The Amazing True Life Story of Mrs. Georgia Anne Layton*, in the summer of 2013.

Made in the USA
Charleston, SC
24 June 2012